Penguin Books
Beautiful

Rachel Billington was born in Oxford in 1942. She was
educated at a Catholic convent and at Oxford University,
where she took a B.A. honours degree in English Literature
and Language. She then went to work in television as a
researcher. In 1965 she moved to New York to work for the
American Broadcasting Corporation on documentary
programmes. Six months' researching drug addiction also
gave background material for her first novel, *All Things Nice*
(1967).

In 1966 she met her husband, film and theatre director Kevin
Billington, in New York and they were married in 1967.
She then concentrated on writing novels, which include
The Big Dipper (1970), *Lilacs Out of the Dead Land*, *Cock Robin*
and *A Painted Devil* (1975). She has also worked on film scripts,
has published various short stories and has recently written
a play, *Mrs Bleasdale's Lodger*, for B.B.C. radio. She spent a
year as book reviewer for *Cosmopolitan*.

The Billingtons have three children.

Rachel Billington

Beautiful
A Modern Romance

Penguin Books

Penguin Books Ltd, Harmondsworth,
Middlesex, England
Penguin Books, 625 Madison Avenue,
New York, New York 10022, U.S.A.
Penguin Books Australia Ltd, Ringwood,
Victoria, Australia
Penguin Books Canada Ltd, 2801 John Street,
Markham, Ontario, Canada L3R 1B4
Penguin Books (N.Z.) Ltd, 182–190 Wairau Road,
Auckland 10, New Zealand

First published by William Heinemann Ltd 1974
Published in Penguin Books 1977
Copyright © Rachel Billington, 1974

Made and printed in Great Britain by
C. Nicholls & Company Ltd,
The Philips Park Press, Manchester
Set in Monotype Baskerville

For Kevin

PART I

'O! she doth teach the torches to burn bright.
It seems she hangs upon the cheek of night
Like a rich jewel in an Ethiop's ear;
Beauty too rich for use, for earth too dear!'

Romeo and Juliet, Act I, scene v

I

Lucy was beautiful. People said it to her constantly. They also said it to each other though then jealousy made them try to criticize. Some added she was so sexy too, which was meant to be catty as her sex life was well known for its richness and variety. But that usually turned out to be a compliment too for she managed her affaires so well that they seemed only the oil to make her life run more smoothly.

So Lucy was beautiful and sexy. It was indisputable. Any man she met spoke of her white bosom and her Mona Lisa pink smile.

As if two such outstanding qualities were not enough, Lucy was also extremely clever. In fact, her cleverness was the root from which her other two attributes sprang. She was born clever. She discovered and developed her sexuality. She made herself beautiful.

Lucy prized her hard-won beauty above all. Because she was naturally clever she thought nothing of her success in conquering the world of Interior Decorating. In the same way it was as easy for her to catch a lover as an expert angler catches a minnow. But her beauty had taken time, energy, planning, money, enthusiasm. She did not achieve it till she was twenty-three – a third of the way through her natural span of years.

Everything Lucy said or did was in the expectation that someone would say how beautiful she looked. 'Lucy is *en grande beauté* tonight.' If two hours passed without such a compliment she felt unhappy, a failure. She was ambitious to be beautiful.

This ambition was not entirely self-centred, for since they were an extension of herself, she wanted her children to be beautiful too, and her house in Hampstead, and her close friends.

Now she looked into the mirror on her dressing-table and was happy. The soft glow of the setting sun through the white lace curtains of her bedroom windows turned her face the most delicious creamy pink, tinged her golden hair with red and made her eyes the deepest sapphire blue. She was glad she had dressed romantically and admired the silky frills round her famous bosom and the dangling earrings under her softly curling hair. She lifted the full length of her white neck and felt with delight the way her thighs lay so gently on the velvet-upholstered chair under the organdie-covered dressing-table.

'You look so beautiful tonight.'

Lucy smiled. That special sweet mysterious smile reserved for this special word, and felt the evening was off to a perfect start.

'Thank you, darling.'

'Can I just push in that hair-pin for you, Mummy?'

'Do, Lizzie.'

Eliza was Lucy's eldest daughter. She was fourteen which meant that Lucy was thirty-six. Lucy found this as hard to believe as everyone else did, but on the whole enjoyed even the tempered compliments which her daughter's appearance evoked, '. . . and considering she has a teenage – ' etc. Lucy had younger children also, but they were not yet so important in her life. Nor she in theirs. They represented nursery life.

Eliza was her acolyte, the high priestess at the temple of beauty, and as befitted such a glorious post, she was herself extremely pretty – if not yet beautiful. She was dark-haired. Her hair was a rich curtain that she sometimes hid behind in childlike self-consciousness, or sometimes flung back like a cloak against her narrow shoulder blades so that her oval face and large blue eyes glowed in shining pink-cheeked innocence. Then people said how like her mother she was and how beautiful she would be.

The two faces were reflected like a Victorian miniature in the dusky mirror. Eliza was serious, with eyes only for the proper presentation of her mother's beauty. Lucy was dreamy, floating ahead to thoughts of what the night would bring.

'There!' exclaimed Eliza.

'Thank you, darling,' said Lucy, rising in a waft of scents and silky material. 'How long and pretty your hair has become.' Eliza blushed and stood back as her mother drifted past.

Downstairs in the drawing-room, Alex was waiting anxiously for Lucy. The drawing-room was an extension of Lucy. As delicately garlanded, as richly coloured, as sweetly scented. Low sofas were piled high with embroidered cushions, velvets patched with silk and patterned with glistening beads. Foot-stools like exotic beetles tiptoed round the carved legs of pin-cushioned chairs. Tables mosaic-topped, gloss over petals, rosewood with delicate strips of satinwood, were decorated like birthday cakes with myriads of tiny boxes, half-cut semi-precious stones and photographs framed in ornate gold or rich Moroccan red or splinters of Venetian glass. Everything was sensuous, individual, Lucy's. Even the flowers, which grew in painted pots from every corner of the room, seemed to breathe some special air which made the lilies linger longer, their great horns flared boldly open to show the delicately spotted interior. An orange tree reflected its medieval leaves and brilliant fruit into the mirror table below so that it became a fairyland orchard. Bright bunches of freesias, their pink and yellow horns as delicate as the lilies were stately, overflowed narrow silver vases and filled the air with a sweet scent. The greyness of London in late autumn seemed a world away.

Alex was dark and tall and managed to look both handsome and upper class – socially, a much sought-after combination. Alex was Lucy's current lover. He seemed very masculine in this flowery bower. Particularly as he was taking long strides up and down the room. He had begun pacing five minutes ago, although he had only arrived three minutes before that. He was always on edge in Lucy's house, for although he had been her lover for over a year he still half expected a pistol shot to ring out. The fact that he was made so welcome by the whole family, husband included, made him feel even more uneasy. However, quite often he confused this disagreeable sense of unease with the delicious but nervous sexual anticipation appropriate to a meeting with Lucy. So now he paced restlessly and thought himself the luckiest man alive.

The door was flung open.

'Mummy's coming!' Eliza cried, who had nipped along ahead to make this announcement. 'She looks so beautiful.'

Eliza stood back to let Lucy enter and watched with admiration as she was kissed warmly on both cheeks by Alex.

'You smell like a ripe peach.'

'Shall I get you a drink?' Eliza could relax a bit now that homage had been properly paid.

'The children haven't been down yet.'

Lucy settled on a sofa, but her eyes were still turning Alex's feet to jelly. 'Any more knives discovered today?'

Even at her most romantic, Lucy enjoyed conversation. The habit had grown on her during the twenty-three years before she had become beautiful, and although now she need only sit quiet and still to command admiration, she could not change her ways. Besides, she really loved witty wicked dialogue of which she herself was the acknowledged mistress. Her reference to knives was an allusion to Alex's profession as a criminal barrister. He was at present involved in a murder case which hinged on the length of the knife used for the murder.

Alex laughed.

'We're having an expert on acupuncture in tomorrow.'

'There must be easier ways.'

'You should see the photographs.'

'Bloody, bloody man.'

By a coincidence that wasn't a coincidence, Lucy's husband, Tom Trevelyan, was also a criminal barrister and, not surprisingly, since he had a thirty-year start on Alex, he was a Queen's Counsel too. Alex was twenty-six, Lucy was thirty-six and Tom was fifty-five.

While Lucy and Alex bandied criminal quips and sexual *coup d'oeils* in his drawing-room, Tom was bent over his desk in his chambers in The Temple. His high forehead, framed by hair, once black but now grey and thinning, topped a long bony nose and a straight thin mouth. His complexion was pale but tinged red at the jawbones as if a more outdoor life would turn it a handsome red colour. He was a distinguished-looking man, with a certain aloofness about him that kept even his closest friends from becoming too personal. He was the sort of successful lawyer who seemed to find each case more absorbing than the last. He seldom arrived home till late and even then had his other interests – the City and a conservation society of which he was chairman. He was a busy man.

The coincidence of similar professions between husband and lover was not a coincidence because it was the reason that Alex and Lucy had met. Tom had introduced them. Alex was in his chambers and a protégé of his. Lucy's last *amour* had been a composer of modern music and Tom was not fond of music beyond the nineteenth century, in which he was rather knowledgeable. Tom had learnt in the first few years of marriage with Lucy that the love and admiration of a husband was not enough for her. It was no reflection on him personally. For some reason there was a bottomless well inside her which craved love like an addict craves heroin. All the time she was trying for the one fix that would satisfy. And some did for a bit and when they wore out she moved on. Tom had been married to her for fifteen years and worshipped her even more than he had at the start.

'Mummy! Mummy! I've stubbed my toe. I've stubbed my toe on the door.'

'Poor darling. Let me see.' Lucy bent her shiny head over her small son's bare foot. This was Rupert, aged six, who had just come running into the drawing-room followed by his three-year-old sister, Ticky, and their nanny, Pauline. Although the smaller children did not come down from the nursery often, Lucy was always extremely affectionate when they did.

Alex sat in his velvet armchair with his drink and admired the pretty picture that Lucy made with her children. Although he had seen it often before, it never failed to impress him and fill him with lewd thoughts because of the exciting contrast between this smiling madonna and the other woman he knew in bed.

'Is your drink all right?' Eliza hovered beside Alex. She always made his gin and tonic for him and took the task very seriously.

'Have a Coke if you want, Lizzie.' Lucy shrugged off Rupert and Ticky, who was stroking her arm, for she tired of the maternal role quicker than her audience's appreciation.

'I don't want a Coke.' Eliza was hurt that her mother

should think her care over Alex's welfare was a hint that she wanted a drink.

'Upstairs, everybody.' Lucy rose and Pauline shepherded her flock upstairs.

'I don't have to go upstairs yet.' Eliza was in sudden rebellion. Lucy capitulated immediately; she detested unpleasantness of any kind. To her the harmony of her drawing-room was sacred and must be disturbed by no whim of her daughters. That was the only principle at stake. In a way she was a liberal mother. She kissed Eliza warmly.

'No. Of course not, darling. You can stay here and welcome Daddy home.'

'Will he be very tired?'

'You can pour him a lovely large Glen Moranje.'

'We'll be late, Lucy.' Alex uncrossed his elegant legs and put his empty glass on the mantelpiece. It stood unattractively among the photographs and pretty knick-knacks so carefully arranged there. Lucy noticed it but said nothing. Again it was a question of the greater harmony.

'Where's my cloak, I wonder?'

'Oh, I'll get it.' Eliza, quite slave-like again, ran away eagerly. Alex and Lucy took the opportunity to kiss more warmly. Lucy emerged looking pinker and younger, as if she had sipped at some elixir of life.

'Good-bye, darling, and don't leave your homework too late.'

Eliza watched from the door as the two handsome figures, one so fair, one so dark, got into the navy blue sports car and drove away. It was October but the air was surprisingly mild. Huge globular hydrangeas still bloomed in the front garden and their Lucy pink was lit up in the street lamps. Eliza fluttered her fingers over one and then returned to the house and the drawing-room. Pouring herself a Coke on the rocks, she took up position on the sofa, fitting herself as much as possible into the curves left by her mother.

*

Alex wanted to snatch Lucy up and drive her away to an enchanted island, or at very least his flat, but as it happened they were on their way to a dinner party.

'Do butter up Lady K.' Lucy put her hand on Alex's thigh. She loved dinner parties but in this one she had an ulterior motive.

'I'll ask to be shown the bedroom at once.'

Lucy giggled. She was at present redesigning their bedroom.

'Isn't that a little subtle?'

'Kill two birds with one stone.' Alex lifted the hand from his leg and might have placed it in an even more exciting position if it had not been gently withdrawn.

'Just reserve your most lurid stories.'

'What! Not the dwarf with the bulldozer ...?'

'No.'

'Nor the blonde with three ...?'

'No.'

'It's a criminal waste!'

*

A butler opened the door of Sir Patrick Keegan's splendid house on Highgate Hill and a maid took their coats from them. At the door to the drawing-room, a waiter offered them a tray of drinks. It was obviously going to be a large party. Lucy chose champagne and moved confidently forward. It was a long time since she had been to a party where more than a handful of the guests were unknown to her. She rather disliked this as her restless intelligence tired of people easily. It was unusual that she had stayed so long with Alex. Knowing everybody was the price she paid for being an energetic hostess herself. Lucy loved entertaining only slightly less than she loved being entertained and did it so well that people wondered how she worked and had children as well – not to mention lovers.

'The young are never energetic.' Sir Patrick Keegan was seventy, a retired Astronomer Royal and his comment was more likely to give himself pleasure than Lucy. They had moved to the dining-room, fourteen at the table and Lucy was on her host's right. The party, it appeared, was in her honour.

'Morton's fork,' she laughed wryly. 'Young and torpid or old and energetic.'

'Ah, but you're the everlasting exception. The last planet in Bode's Law.'

'Are stars much more interesting than people?'

'Of course.'

'I thought so. So much more perfect; so much more . . .' Lucy would have said beautiful if Sir Patrick with the haphazard sense of timing due to age had not interrupted her.

'Religion does for some. Gives that sense of exaltation.'

'Religion comes in all shapes and sizes.' Lucy looked reflective and her silky pink lips quivered, as if about to express some further more complicated thought.

'Lucy's a Holy Roman, you know. Church every Sunday,' Alex almost shouted.

He was seated on Lucy's left and had leant right across her to deliver this piece of information. Sir Patrick was a little put out by such a crude interruption; but to an old man, one conversation is much the same as another.

'Of course, of course. I'd forgotten for a moment. I hope your hard-working husband's coming later, I have a legal conundrum for him.'

Lucy was quite definitely put out. She did not like Alex's possessive interference; nor his rancorous tone. Tom never spoke to her or about her in that irreverent way. She frowned and then, unwilling to admit he had ruffled her perfect serenity, covered it with a sweet but impersonal smile. She inclined her head slightly in the way a queen appears to listen when she is really thinking of her pet corgis. It was no coincidence that the mention of Lucy's Catholicism had reminded Sir Patrick of her husband. Tom loved his religion. On weekdays his well-tailored figure stood out nobly at the altar rails, otherwise barely filled by a few old ladies. Religion was much more to him than a Sunday observance. It was part of his attitude, his sense of the fundamentals of life, of the romance, and one of the reasons why he would never break with Lucy. Not that he feared the wrath of the Church but because its insistence on rocklike continuity and order accorded with his own nature.

This was what gave him his strength and what others sensed when they hesitated to deride him as the foolishly cuckolded husband.

Tom had a special devotion for the Virgin Mary.

*

In fact, Sir Patrick would not be disappointed, for Tom did intend to put in an appearance at the party, but first was giving time to his daughter, Eliza. He was at home playing draughts with her. They sat on the sofa in the softly glowing drawing-room with the board between them. Eliza had put on her pyjamas and her dark hair streamed over a red Viyella dressing-gown. She was sucking the end of the cord reflectively.

Tom, who looked tired but relaxed, had stripped to his shirtsleeves and between moves sipped at his Glen Moranje.

The lines which creased his forehead had disappeared in the company of his daughter.

Eliza looked at the board distractedly.

'I wish I was brilliantly clever.'

'Much better not.' Tom took two of her pieces in a row. 'Much better for girls to be good at sewing and singing.'

'Oh, Daddy, you don't really think that?'

'Why not? Girls should be seen and not heard.'

Eliza looked up at him, blue eyes glistening, 'Then why did you marry Mummy?' Her voice rose triumphantly.

Tom smiled, 'Who said you weren't clever?'

Eliza sighed, 'Well, no one at school says I am, so I can't be.'

'Perhaps they just don't think of telling you.'

'Mummy always tells me when I look pretty. You always tell me when you like something I've done.'

'That's because we're your parents.'

Tom adored his family, although with Lucy adoration merged with admiration; he considered her so far superior to other women as to be another species. Each child had a special place in his love; Eliza was the first creation of his union with Lucy and perhaps a reminder of a time when she had still looked only to him; Rupert was his son, his heir and promise of the continuity of a future; while Ticky was the baby who could still be played with like a doll. If Tom had not been so involved with his work and his other outside interests, he might have seemed more of a family man than his wife. He himself, although an only child, had come from a spreading Scottish family of cousins, uncles and aunts. Before his marriage, he had bought a house in Scotland to which they moved in the school holidays. And there, in his own domain, he felt most at ease. If the sophisticated wonderland of their

London house was Lucy's natural setting, Ardlochray, a solid granite house, was his. He needed to warm himself against a fire that burned pine logs cut from the pine forests he had played in as a boy. He loved to set out, face against the wind, with a gun under his arm. That way he could survive the cramped offices of London, the crowded drawing-rooms.

He stood up rather grimly. Scotland was where he felt most himself and was also most removed from a fashionable London dinner party. But duty must be done.

'Sorry, Lizzie.'

'Bedtime, I know.' Eliza jumped up and gave him a hug. 'Have a good time. Mummy looked absolutely gorgeous!'

Tom smiled at her enthusiasm. 'Of course.'

*

The dinner party had reached the pudding course. Lucy, whose appetite for life did not exclude food, was enjoying an orange soufflé. She was the subject of a conversation across the table between a parody of a Russian émigré – his bone structure resembled the Eiffel Tower – and a dark wry-faced girl. Chloe said:

'Don't expect me to criticize Lucy.'

'But how charming!' Ivanov's voice was a curious mixture of Russian, English and American. It showed the strata of his varied life.

'I wish my husband were so amenable.' A silly-faced girl smiled at the ageing roué who replied by an elegant lift of the eyebrow.

'Tom is a fascinating man.' Chloe would have seemed passionate without the mocking tone that was habitual with her. 'A man in his own right.'

Ivanov raised the other eyebrow.

'My dear young lady, I don't think we've met before.'

'Chloe's a photographer. A liberated woman.' The silly girl smiled again.

'Ah.'

'Not Lesbian,' said Chloe suddenly. But it would have taken much more to disturb Ivanov.

'Ah,' he murmured again.

'There's so many about these days. And with my short hair ...' Although Chloe appeared so tart and outspoken, she often let her sentences unravel gently at the end. She was, at the moment, in the difficult position of being both Lucy's best friend and Alex's sister. Like Alex, she was dark and handsome with strong features accentuated by the way her hair was cropped around her ears. Unlike her brother she was small and slight and moved with impatient speed, as if irritated by other people's slowness. In fact she was the perfect foil for Lucy's generous beauty, although it would have been unfair to suggest that that was why Lucy chose her as a friend, since they had in common a tremendous enthusiasm for their work, and Lucy employed Chloe in her capacity as a photographer. In their roles of mistress and confidante they spoke on the telephone almost every morning, even if they weren't planning to meet. Chloe, whose love life and career were in a constant state of flux, admired Lucy and despaired of ever being like her. She admired her most for her powers of organization, secondly for her religious belief and thirdly for her husband. All the men Chloe liked were married. And although she was eight years younger than Lucy, she already felt life was slipping her by.

'And is her business good?' Ivanov, despite or because of his distinguished air, was part of what might be vulgarly called a P.R.O. service in New York. Lucy, whom he had known in a social setting for many years, could benefit from his promotion.

'Of course,' Chloe laughed. That was an easy one. 'Go up and see her bedroom.'

'Does she only do bedrooms?'

*

The dinner was over by the time Tom arrived and more guests had appeared to fill the drawing-room. Nevertheless, Lady Keegan, who had a vacuous eye for all but distinguished guests, spotted him instantly.

'Tom, dear. We missed you at dinner.'

Tom looked across the room until he found Lucy who sat on a crimson chair like a queen among courtiers. Lady Keegan exclaimed:

'As beautiful as ever.'

'But yours is "a green and smiling age".'

'Gallant as always.'

Tom smiled, 'A lawyer must have a good memory.'

'But not necessarily for Shakespeare.'

'When the right subject presents itself.' And then Lady Keegan had to let him go.

Tom stood in front of Lucy. She smiled up at him as he bent to kiss her cheek. Her smile was warm and true but quite different from the curling lips that made Alex tremble.

'What a long day.'

'These Queen's Counsels.' Alex crooked his head upwards.

'I'm only staying for a moment,' said Tom. He looked at Alex too with a friendly expression but casually as if, perhaps, he were a younger brother. Liked, even loved, but of no tremendous significance. His real attention was for Lucy. He had come to see she was happy and to preserve the conventions. Now he would leave.

'Oh, darling.'

Lucy mouthed regret.

'Is it fun?'

'Well.'

'Alex will bring you home then.'

Tom made his way out of the party, stopping for a moment with Chloe and then listening slightly impatiently to a Member of Parliament who wanted his advice on a case of libel.

'Ring me,' he said, 'in chambers.' He had never been a social person.

Lucy was enjoying herself. As she always did when there were enough balls in the air. She had arranged to have lunch the next day with Ivanov which could be productive for American expansion, she had met a young set designer who seemed already besotted – sometimes she minded her reputation going before her in this way – and Alex was hovering impatiently, desirously behind her.

'What is the colour of tension?' The set designer was called Darrell and had pushed his way into the circles of success by his superior flow of adrenalin.

'Silver,' Lucy suggested.

'That's not a colour.' Alex left them to find another drink. Normally he could be relied upon to be generously courteous to Lucy's other admirers – always a legion – for, after all, he was in possession, but tonight he was irritable. Lucy did not watch him go but continued the conversation with Darrell as if it had not been interrupted.

'I've always been fascinated by the use of colour to create a mood. Most people get no further than green for restfulness yet for a stage designer ...?' She trailed off and looked with flattering inquiry at Darrell. He was not slow to take up the challenge. He worked as hard to impress the lovely Lucy Trevelyan as he would for a stageful of directors.

Nevertheless, on this occasion at least, Alex prevailed and by one-thirty he had captured Lucy for himself. But his victory was insecure. They stood in Berkeley Square and almost argued. Alex wanted to take Lucy back to his flat and Lucy, invigorated by the party, wanted to go into the night club, Annabel's.

'But I thought you enjoyed showing me off.'

'In the old days.'

'The old days?' Lucy grimaced at the unfortunate image.

Inside the night club, as was inevitable, they found more friends – or rather Lucy did – and it was three o'clock before she allowed herself to be led out. Alex was tired but Lucy was as pink-cheeked as ever and at last she was ready for his flat. The visit, as usual, was a success.

Alex's flat was as impersonal as any conventional middle-class bachelor's, yet its two rooms, bedroom and living-room, mirrored his interests. In the one he worked, so that piles of briefs, notebooks and law volumes lay around tables and floor, and in the other he made love and, as a subsidiary occupation, slept, so there was a splendid bed with purple quilted eiderdown and shiny brass railings. The Knightsbridge decorator, whose taste in *eau de nil* brocade and regency stripes had depressed so many, never failed with this sumptuous, spongy bed.

Now Lucy and Alex stood on either side of it. Alex's love, even adoration of Lucy had never been a bar to their making love in the jolliest ways. Lucy, true to her gourmet nature, enjoyed the moments of anticipation so much that she might have seemed a tease were she not so generous later with her gifts. She pulled a curl to her mouth and made her eyes gape as if she were some eighteenth-century romp.

'I've got a riddle.'

'With a happy ending, I hope.'

'Oh, yes.'

Lucy began to pluck off her jewellery and toss it onto the bed. Alex circled her, reaching first to his tie and then to her rounded shoulder. She untied her dress at the shoulders.

'What are tied with pink ribbons?'

'Babies' bootees.'

Lucy giggled and her dress rippled to the floor. 'Cold. Cold.'

'Love letters.' Alex tore at his shirt, at his trousers, made a preparatory lunge at Lucy's succulent hip.

'Getting warmer.'

Alex stood in his underpants. Lucy, naked now – her pink breasts pressing eagerly between her arms, was crouching on the bed; with playful fingers, she swooped towards him.

'That's a hint!' she cried, trying to snatch at the waistband. And her rounded buttocks came uppermost, bobbing, dimpled. Alex watched, face flushed, but played the game.

'Ah! I have it. A barrister's briefs.'

Nimbly he stepped out of his pants and flung them in the air. 'Now I've a riddle for you. What's a barrister without his briefs?' He stood in front of her, nude, proud, gloriously erect.

'Oh dear, oh dear.' Lucy wriggled humbly among the bedclothes in mock despair, 'I'll never get that one.'

'Oh yes, you will,' Alex bounded up onto the bed. 'He's a man!'

'Oh Alex, Alex!' Lucy cried and then became softer and quieter till the bed's luxurious squeaking was the only noise.

2

But the next morning Lucy was not so sure that the evening had been a success – for her, that is. Alex's rancorous tone at the dinner table stayed disagreeably in mind. Besides, he had argued with her in Berkeley Square.

She lay back among a pile of pillows in her own gauzy bed and thought how much more fun he'd been in the summer. Even the vision of her bedroom which was papered with pale cabbage roses and trimmed with turquoise velvet curtains and skirted chairs failed to soothe her spirits. She lifted her eyes to the gigantic crystal ball suspended above her head and saw her face repeated a thousand times. She felt an unacceptable lassitude. There was a knock at the door.

'Morning, Mummy.' 'Morning, Mummy.' 'Good morning, Mrs Trevelyan.' 'Good morning, ma'am.' The younger children, their nanny and Maria with her breakfast tray came into the room. Lucy gracefully accepted their kisses, her bed jacket, her tray, the light as they drew back the curtains, but remained abstracted. She waved Maria away as she hovered behind the others.

'I'll order later.' Instead she pressed the 'on' button on her telephone which immediately rang.

'Chloe . . . It was, I suppose. But what has happened to Alex?'

Whatever answer Chloe gave, it did not satisfy Lucy who was as irritated by ambiguous behaviour as a lawyer. There was no doubt Alex worshipped her. Then why did he not stay on his knees?

'In the summer. In Scotland, he felt no need to prove himself in this childish manner.'

Lucy and Chloe both thought about the summer in Scotland. Scotland was another of Lucy's triumphs. At the start of her marriage their visits had seemed a boring wifely duty which she performed for Tom as graciously as possible. But Lucy could never do anything half-heartedly and gradually that 'graciously as possible' began to take over. Soon Scotland was drawn into her glorious orbit – in a different style as befitted the wild north, but just as compelling. The house and the grounds, subdued to her will in the shape of herb gardens, rose gardens, tennis courts, sauna, paddocks for pony and boating lake, became a pleasure ground for herself, her friends and her lovers. If Tom ever felt his family home invaded, he never showed it and rather seemed delighted that Lucy was so much happier to spend time in the part of the earth he loved most. After all, she had made the effort for his sake in the first place.

Now Lucy sighed with the memories of delightful summer activities.

Chloe, who was sitting in her kitchen wrapped in a large towelling robe with a cup of coffee, had a photograph on the wall as a reminder. She had taken it herself one hot day when they had picnicked beside the loch. She had been lying down so that the water stretched away at eye level. Sleepy, rather drunk after a lot of wine in beakers, she had taken the picture out of focus. If anything, Chloe thought wryly, it celebrated Lucy's triumphant energy. For Lucy was in the icy loch. She had jumped to her feet after a small siesta.

'Who's in with me?'

'Oh, no.' Chloe rolled on her back.

'You can't. Oh, Mummy,' Eliza wailed. 'I haven't brought a bathing suit.'

'Neither have I. Nymphs and shepherds come away . . .'
Lucy danced over to a small cluster of silver birch trees
and started to pull off her clothes.

'Do let's,' said Eliza's friend, Jessica.

'You're all mad,' Edwina and Mungo, Lucy's guests who
were not living up to expectations, groaned in horror.
Tom read his *Financial Times* peacefully and far away down
the loch Alex cast a line. Some of this was in the photograph.

'You had more time for him in Scotland,' Chloe said
daringly.

'He was more fun.'

The water had been icy cold but Lucy had tripped
lightly into it as if it were asses' milk. Behind her Eliza and
Jessica shrieked and splashed. Eliza with youthful modesty
had kept on pants and T-shirt.

Lucy swam quietly upstream till she was ten yards or so
from Alex.

'Mermaids ahoy!' she cried.

Alex waved his rod. 'Swim nearer. You're my only
hope of a catch.' He made as if to cast and Lucy who had
obeyed his summons stood up in imagined alarm. A flurry
of water spread up round her like a magic cloak and then
ran off her body in glistening drops.

'Aphrodite from the waves.' Alex stared admiringly.

There was a loud splash further up the loch.

'Tom's in!' said Alex, looking beyond Lucy who
dropped back into the water and swam briskly round to
where her husband had dived off a bank.

'Pretty mermaid,' he said, as she approached him. At
which she ducked and rolled gaily like a seal.

Meanwhile the girls were getting cold.

'Bbbrrhh.' Eliza scrambled out with soaking T-shirt
clinging to her childishly pointed breasts. But Jessica,
naked as Lucy, stood up boldly.

'Jessica. He's looking. Alex is looking,' Eliza hissed through shivering teeth.

Chloe had lain and watched it all and taken her photographs. Occasionally during that summer, she had occupied herself by wondering if she was in love with Tom whose rangy tweediness and hawklike face were so impressive among his native crags, but mostly she thought of him as 'the High Priest' in the temple of Lucy's beauty. Lucy had been blithely flirtatious in the summer holidays, like a young girl.

'I do hate jealousy,' said Lucy into the telephone. 'Alex is even jealous of my work.'

'That's True Love.'

'No. It's not. It's selfish greed.'

'Hard words.'

'Hold on, the other line's ringing.' Lucy pressed a button. 'Hello ... How prompt ... indeed. *Malheureusement*, I'm already lunching ...' The flattering conversation drifted on. Chloe made herself another cup of coffee; she didn't mind hanging on; it was rather restful.

'That was Darrell. That designer from last night.'

'He's very successful.'

'He knows a fantastic warehouse filled with imported silks.'

'Ah. Alex cut off my pet mouse's tail.'

'I've never felt much sympathy with mice.'

After Chloe rang off, Lucy lay back for a moment. In order to lead a day of unremitting energy, she had to have this moment of tranquillity. It struck her that Eliza had not come up to say her usual good morning. It was important to Lucy's well-being that the household kept to a strict routine, so that she knew that everything and everybody was working smoothly. She buzzed the nursery.

'Eliza didn't come up this morning.'

'She went to school early, Mrs Trevelyan.'

So that was all right. Lucy smiled; Eliza was so beautiful and clever and adored her so much. Eliza also adored Alex. Lucy knew that she made each of her lovers into a hero for her family and, though not a conscious policy, she liked it, for after all she had taken him up to the pinnacle with her. She thought of the way Eliza danced attendance on Alex and smiled again. It was almost puppy love. The idea flattered her and when the phone rang her good humour was nearly restored.

'Good morning . . . I'm lunching with Ivanov . . . but it's work, Alex . . . Come and have a nursery tea instead.'

Her heart softened further with the sound of his voice. Memories of the night before, of his youthful good looks, in particular of his elegant long legs wound round her so securely, filled her imagination. She smiled at herself. Besides, generally, he had such an air of old-world gallantry; so near the image of a 'veray parfait gentilhom'. It had been unlike her to exaggerate her emotions. What, after all, was a little petty temper? She jumped lightly out of bed and went to the long bathroom mirror. She drew her nightdress over her head. Was she changing in other ways? No. Her body was as smooth and white as ever, despite her three children; not delicately undeveloped like Eliza's or Eliza's friend Jessica, but mature and vigorous. Lucy smoothed her tummy gently. Jessica was not really clever enough, beautiful enough for her daughter. She suspected the main attraction was her home background, which was murky and excited Eliza's childish imagination. How extraordinary youth was in this way. She supposed Jessica was the price one must pay for democracy. And yet, why should she lower her standards for some nebulous principle? Lucy began to think of the importance of friends and soon came to the conclusion that the only rule was the attraction of opposites. So if the pretty virginal Eliza wanted the dingy, slightly vulgar Jessica, she must have her and she, Lucy, must direct her efforts into raising Jessica into a new, more glittering orbit, rather than tearing apart the relationship. Nothing was worth an ugly severing. One must never deny! With this happy resolution, she stepped towards the shower.

*

'Darling. So beautiful!'

'Ivy. You old flatterer.'

They kissed in the foyer of the Connaught Hotel. Lucy had come from her office where she had put in two good hours of work; Ivanov from his bed.

'Champagne?'

'I'm a working woman.'

'All the more reason.'

One of Ivanov's main attributes was his ability to command the best table in any restaurant, so Lucy was perfectly placed to see Alex when he entered the room. Her wide blue eyes with their darkened lashes gazed at him over her champagne glass. Beside him was Chloe.

'All that panelling and tasselling makes New York like a bourgeois club,' Ivanov was saying.

'Book fronts and occasional tables,' murmured Lucy. But her socially orientated friend was too sharp for any dissemblance. He followed her gaze.

'Aha.'

'Hello, darling,' said Alex.

'He stabbed my goldfish,' said Chloe.

'Alex and Chloe Beardsley.'

'But last night . . .' Ivanov kissed Chloe's hand. 'Though I didn't realize you were *sposata*.' His eyes flickered to Lucy.

'Our mother was.'

'Your mother. Ah.' Ivanov looked disappointed; Lucy, from behind her iron smile, irritated; Chloe amused and Alex determined. 'Perhaps we could come together again over coffee.' Ivanov was less keen to share his beautiful guest now that the situation was less shocking. Lucy's smile was as sweet as cough linctus.

'I have tea at lunchtime.'

*

At tea-time her attitude was unchanged. Alex, who had been waiting for her in the dusky flower-smelling drawing-room, failed hopelessly to place a kiss on her bright cold face.

'I said a nursery tea. With the children for the children.'

'My case finished early. I wanted to see you.'

'I haven't even seen Tom today.'

'Last night . . .'

Lucy turned angrily and went to the door, 'was last night. Now, are you coming up to the nursery?' She left him no choice, for she was already running up the stairs; her kilted skirt swung round her long legs. When Lucy found a situation in which she felt justifiable anger, very few could withstand her. The contrast between her usually serene face and her sudden pointed vehemence was intolerable. All anyone wanted was to restore her beauty. Alex followed her slowly up the stairs and the silver tracery leaves on the high walls, which usually seemed so filled with light, had turned to prison bars. Luckily, Lucy herself had always a strong wish to restore goodwill, so when she stood at the nursery door and saw the happy scene there, all her ill-humour disappeared into maternal appreciation. How pretty they looked, Rupert, Ticky and their young nanny, Pauline, sitting round the kitchen table.

'I shot two goals today,' boasted Rupert. 'With my left foot. Like Pele.'

'Did you, darling? You are clever. And what did you do, Ticky?'

'I – I drwooo a pictuuuure.' Ticky had the most fetching lisp imaginable that made anyone laugh to hear it.

'Darling,' said Lucy, hugging her and then taking the chair at her side. Alex settled on a sofa where he found a brightly coloured jack-in-the-box. He pressed the button experimentally.

'Wheeeooww.'

'Alex is not allowed to press Ticky's jack,' Rupert groused.

'Don't be so bossy, darling.' Lucy's mood had progressed beyond the limits of childish virtues and back to the grown-up male. She smiled at Alex bewitchingly who replied by pressing the jack once more. Its ludicrous face with black button eyes, leering scarlet lips and jester's cap lurched towards her.

*

Outside in the street Eliza was swinging her way home from school. Beside her walked Jessica who she was bringing back for tea. Although they looked alike with long un-brushed hair, coloured tights and box jackets, they were as different as chalk from cheese for Eliza was still a child in all her attitudes and emotions and Jessica had already progressed into the trickier waters of adolescence. This was something that Lucy in her morning analysis had not precisely realized. They stopped outside the house.

'Come on, then,' said Eliza. 'It's getting parky.'

'Is your mother in?'

'I expect so.' Eliza looked up at the nursery window. 'She usually is for tea.'

'Let's go straight to your room.'

'But tea's upstairs.'

'She makes me feel so silly. As if my pants might fall down.'

Eliza looked at her with surprise.

'Mummy! But she's always lovely to you.'

'Gracious.'

'I think you're being very rude.'

Jessica capitulated.

'I'm sorry, Eliza. It's just, I don't know ... I expect I'm jealous. You know when Daddy went ...'

'Oh, Jessie.' Eliza saw her point immediately. 'It must have been dreadful. I mean a father's so important, however much you love your mother.' Nevertheless, she looked up at the window eagerly as a loud laugh descended. 'Alex is up there too. Come on.'

Once more Jessica hung back, but this time her sulky expression overlay a certain excitement. However she said,

'Wouldn't it be cosy? Just the two of us? Downstairs.'

'Rightiho!' Eliza was disappointed but felt it her duty to humour Jessica in her unhappy circumstances. She took one more look upwards and was rewarded by Alex's dark shadow as he crossed the window.

'I thought you liked Alex,' she couldn't resist saying once they had settled themselves cosily in her bedroom, which was in the basement of the large house. 'You seemed to in Scotland.' For some reason, she, like Chloe, recalled Jessica's nude swim. Her blue eyes behind their curtain of dark hair peered at Jessica, rather embarrassed for her friend.

'You're so pretty,' Jessica evaded her question. 'I don't know why I'm not jealous of you.'

But Eliza had inherited her mother's single-mindedness.

'I think Alex is just about perfect. Handsome, clever, charming. Why are all the boys we know so awful?'

'You're such a hero-worshipper. Honestly, you should be more pragmatic.'

'What?'

'Pragmatic. It means matter of fact.' Jessica looked pleased with herself, since although she was a year older it was usually Eliza who had to explain things to her.

There was a knock at the door.

'Is it girls only?' Alex put his head round the door. Eliza who was sitting on the floor jumped up welcomingly.

'Step right up. A penny a throw. Ten for six pence.'

'I don't think I could manage it.'

Jessica, who had taken up a more languorous pose on the bed at Alex's entrance, giggled knowingly.

'What's that?' Alex wagged his finger at her. 'Naughty chuckles from little girls.'

'Why aren't you upstairs?' Eliza had understood no innuendo. 'Aren't you taking Mummy out?'

'Your mother's chucked me out.'

'She couldn't.' Eliza looked tragic.

'She's going out with a character called Darrell.'

Eliza was puzzled, 'I don't know him.'

'He's a designer. A stage designer. She met him last night. He's taking her to a production of *A Midsummer Night's Dream* which he designed himself. He's very successful.'

'Still, you'll be here tomorrow. For the dinner party,' said Eliza anxiously.

'Oh, yes. A bad penny.'

'Don't be silly.'

Jessica watched them and fingered her long straight hair. When Alex went to the door she swung her legs off the bed.

'Want a lift?' said Alex.

'Yes, please.'

'But Jessie ... I thought we were going to learn that poem together.'

Eliza looked after her reproachfully. But after all she quite understood why anyone would rather have a drive in super Alex's super car than learn boring old Milton. Sighing, she found the dog-eared book of *Paradise Lost*.

*

Upstairs, Lucy lay in her bath. She was wondering about bathroom design; it seemed to her essential that a room constantly filling with hot vapour must be well ventilated, and yet how often did one find a bathroom with an extra large window? It was probably due to the general obsession about peeping Toms. As far as she was concerned anyone could look at her in the bath.

'Come in.'

Eliza came round the door in a rather preoccupied manner and settled on a cane-seated chair. *Paradise Lost* had been abandoned. It was their time-honoured moment for a mother-daughter heart-to-heart.

'Why did you send Alex away, Mummy? He was quite miserable.'

'I haven't sent him away, darling. He'll be back to-morrow.'

'He was quite miserable,' repeated Eliza, the memory of Alex's strained face still before her.

'He was playing at it,' Lucy suggested and instinctively prepared to divert attention to herself. 'What shall I wear tonight, darling? I haven't an idea. Do help me choose ...'

Eliza's large blue eyes which had been cast anxiously down raised in a new sort of concern. She loved choosing her mother's evening outfits.

'How about that blue patterned dress?'

'The one with the Chinesey men on it?'

'Yup. And the red shoes,'

'And the red shawl.'

They smiled at each other and Eliza disappeared happily into the bedroom to lay out the clothes. After a moment she called gaily, 'You are lucky going to *A Midsummer Night's Dream*. We're going to do it at school next term.'

Lucy eyed her finger nails meditatively; she would paint them red. She turned her head sideways so that Eliza would hear her. 'Apparently, the fairies swing from trapezes. Like pretty monkeys.'

'How fantastic!'

'Darrell's idea. The man who's taking me to it.'

'How terrific! He must be terribly successful.'

*

Darrell, who was not yet seriously under Lucy's spell, was a little late arriving that night. Eliza let him in and took him to the drawing-room. She eyed him interestedly; she thought his greying hair rather thrilling on a man still obviously in his twenties, and although his face was too odd-looking to be conventionally handsome – his cheekbones were slavic and his forehead low – there was an air of success and authority about him that without identifying, she liked. Besides he was the most trendy man who had been in the house. There was only one major drawback and this she registered overpoweringly as she came closer to him: he was short. He was short *and* thickset. A snobbishness which told her men should be tall and casual like her father and Alex rose to bar Darrell from her heart. She would remain faithful to the aristocratic length of Alex.

'Do the fairies come from a circus?' she asked politely.

Darrell did not realize the importance that Lucy attached to good relations between her family and her lover. But then he was as yet only on the prospective list. Not bothering to answer Eliza's question, he looked round the beautiful but as far as he was concerned empty room and asked,

'Where's your mother?'

Eliza looked at the floor, 'She'll be down.'

Darrell sat; he stretched his velveteen legs in front of him; he flicked at his long shirt collars. Eliza remained standing. At last something in her attitude struck him.

'We're late, you see,' he said almost placatingly, 'and I particularly wanted your mother to see the opening.'

'I'll call her,' Eliza relented slightly. 'She's kissing Rupert.' Darrell looked so startled that Eliza relented even further, 'My little brother. He expects to be kissed good night.'

'Ah.' Left to himself Darrell eyed his fashionably chiselled features in the mirror above the mantelpiece and then decided to use the room's decoration in his next design of a drawing-room comedy. Though this might not have seemed a compliment to Lucy, in fact it was the highest accolade. He was counting the bottles and type represented on the drinks table when the phone rang. As it went on for some time under his elbow and he was of that free and easy generation who think nothing of picking up other people's telephones, he said casually,

'Hello?'

'Is Mrs Trevelyan there?'

'I hope so. Who's speaking?'

'Mr Trevelyan.'

This threw Darrell.

Later that evening as they drove away from his, quote, 'magnificent *Dream*' in his new Mercedes, he said as much to Lucy.

'What do you mean?' Lucy looked disdainful. Darrell tried to explain his feelings of incongruity but met such an impenetrable silence that he faltered, although usually after watching his production nothing could stop his god-like flow.

'Mustard seed was rather bustless,' said Lucy conversationally.

'Boys are,' replied Darrell and smiling at his restored superiority decided in future to stay off the subject of personal emotions.

Lucy who had been impressed by the evening's entertainment nevertheless thought wistfully of Alex's well-bred understanding of things. She had never had to freeze off presumptuous questions in such a distasteful way. She hoped Darrell was going to be worth it.

'Here we are.' The Mercedes was stopping under a shiny new block of flats. Lucy looked up the gleaming front of glass; it was so different from her own white bow-fronted house. 'And I'm at the top,' said Darrell.

'Of course.' Lucy laughed breathily at the excitement of a new venture and as she stirred her sweet scent filled Darrell's nostrils. The obvious expense of it stimulated him even more than its sexuality.

*

Alex also went out that night but the evening was only a partial success. For one thing, it ended at eleven-thirty; it simply died out in a way that nothing did when Lucy was part of it. The girl he had picked up at a cocktail party was so lifeless; pretty enough, but dull. Besides, she too obviously thought him a desirable catch. The idea of making love to her had filled him with boredom. In future he would go for clever ugly girls. He sighed and images of Lucy's creamy beauty filled him with restless energy. Like many another, he wondered how she could be beautiful, clever, sexy and maternal. For a moment he thought of Eliza and her friend, Jessica. All part of the well-oiled machine that was Lucy's life. Bitterly he decided that she ran her household like a business, nothing must upset it. Certainly no mere lover could compete with her home in her scale of priorities. His irritable state spurring him onto action, he marched determinedly from his flat.

*

'I'm a loner.' Darrell lay on his floor and stared at the ceiling. It was garlanded with giant silver chains from which fierce spikes slanted. Like his Mercedes, the flat was new and a source of pride. Lucy curled up beside him on a sack-cloth cushion and listened with apparent appreciation. He had already explained the special plaster process which made the chains look so genuinely heavy and was now explaining the progress of his own career. Lucy was not simulating interest. New experiences made her happy in a way nothing else did. Besides, she really wanted to know how Darrell had worked his way up to his success and she found his forthright manner less acerbic in the mellower hours of night.

'Have you ever done any stage design?' He turned to Lucy suddenly.

'No. No, I haven't.' Lucy had forgotten her own career for the moment and was therefore slightly surprised by his question. 'I'm a social decorator.'

'You're better than that.' Darrell stared up intensely. 'You're good.'

'I didn't know you'd seen anything I've done.' Lucy smiled lazily.

'I've seen your house. I've seen a book of yours.'

'*The History of the Staircase*. Hardly thrilling.'

'No. *Four Walls and a Man*.'

'Oh, you saw that, did you? I thought they only printed enough to go round my friends.'

'Everyone read it at college.'

'Oh.' Lucy was flattered yet oddly displeased. It made her seem so very much older. Perhaps, after all, she was not going to be swept off her feet by her host.

'You're the most beautiful woman I've ever met,' announced Darrell without warning. His hand went out to Lucy's hair.

'Aah.' Lucy's lips curled into a perfect cupid's bow. In the daytime she wanted to command admiration and respect, but at night she became an odalisque in whose eyes men looked and became mad with desire. She saw that look now start in Darrell's face and her body flowed in warm preparation. She snuggled down into the spongy cushion and watched his rather short-fingered hands spread on either side of her face. She put her hand up to his chest and was startled by its hardness.

'Are you a boxer?' she whispered, as he pressed down towards her.

But Darrell couldn't speak. The ecstasy of having spread out before him all that Lucy represented to his ambitious mind had silenced him. His heart thudded so hard against the chest that Lucy had touched that he had to take action. Suddenly he rolled Lucy, still swathed in silk, so that she lay face-down on the floor. Then he flung himself on top of her.

'Oh!' cried Lucy, surprised and thrilled.

'God,' said Darrell through gritted teeth, for now he had her securely beneath him. 'You snobbish glorious decadent bitch.' Holding a fistful of hair in one hand he began to roll off her dress with the other.

'Ah,' the breath came out of Lucy's body with a soft sigh and she felt herself deliciously mastered. What more was there to life?

*

Tom was chairman at a conservation meeting that evening. The society was addressed by a visiting American who was so dedicated to the cause that even the most serious members became fretful. As chairman, Tom took the full strain of the speaker's verbosity and the audience's impatience, so that when it finally broke up, he drove home quite exhausted.

The cook, Maria, opened the door and switched on the lights for him in the empty drawing-room.

'Madam has said you will have cold dinner.'

'Heat me up some soup, too, would you.'

'Yes, sir, certainly. You have it here, sir?'

'Yes. Yes.'

Tom reached for the evening paper and leant back with relief. It did not occur to him to wish for Lucy's presence. Even at the beginning of their marriage it had been clear to him that he could not expect someone like her to hang around all evening for him. She had never said anything to him about it, but to his lawyer's logical mind it was obvious that a woman like her must choose her own path. He might expect certain things of her; her love and wifely support; her love and care for the children and her care of the house; and in these she was far more generous and successful than most women. In return it was his duty to respect her soul, her privacy. If he wished it otherwise, he never allowed it to show, unless perhaps in the remoteness that people always noted about him. Although always attractive to women, he had been over forty when he married and Lucy was the love of his life. He would never look at another woman. His object, above all, was to keep

Lucy happy and beautiful. On her happiness rested his. If he could not do it alone then she must have others who could. This was far more important to him than any crude convention of the cuckold.

A thought struck him. He got up and went down the stairs to Eliza's room. But no light came from under the door. She must be asleep. Satisfied, he moved quietly away. Inside the room, Eliza, half-woken by his presence, turned over in bed and knocked the book she had been reading, *Anna Karenina*, to the floor.

At about eleven-thirty, after his simple supper, Tom went upstairs and to his own dressing-room where he usually slept. Rather irritated, he saw the curtains had been left undrawn and went across to the window. He couldn't help noticing a man's figure standing on the pavement below the house, as if a sentinel. Without looking further, he firmly shut the heavy damask and turned away.

Alex should have seen the light and the shadow but he was too preoccupied with his own thoughts. He paced up and down and he could see Lucy's face more clearly than her house.

Several times he stopped completely, as when Tom had seen him, and once he thought of Chloe for a moment. Her mocking sisterly tones, 'But Alex, what do you want from her? She's giving you everything she has to offer.' Angrily he paced off again.

It was two or three hours before a Mercedes came slowly up the street; it stopped some yards short of the house. Five minutes went by and then Lucy stepped out gaily and ran up to her front door. She was just inserting her key when she felt a hand on her shoulder.

'Oh!' She turned round, startled but not afraid on her own doorstep. 'Oh, it's you.'

At once Alex saw the futility of his position. 'I was

passing,' he murmured, looking beyond her polite inquiring face.

'How friendly. Late, though,' Lucy smiled.

'Yes. I just wanted . . .'

'Tomorrow, don't you think?' She turned the key.

'Lucy!'

'Sssshhh.' She looked up anxiously. 'You'll wake the whole house.'

'And that would be a disaster.'

'Alex.'

'I'm sorry. I'm going.'

'Tomorrow's today.' Lucy consoled and kissed him lightly on his cheek for his good behaviour. Alex started down the steps but had to turn once more.

'Did you have a good evening?' he cried.

Lucy put her finger to her lips and then changed it to a kiss. It blew off her pearly finger tips to Alex and with that he had to be content.

3

The doorbell first rang at eight o'clock. There was then a pause till eight-thirty, when it rang again. From then on it hardly stopped till the last guest arrived at nine. Lucy liked giving big dinner parties because, unlike most people, she felt her best on formal occasions when the elegance of the surroundings and the elegance of the guests made each want to perform to his utmost.

It was Alex who had arrived early. He straightened his black tie in the hall mirror and then ran upstairs. But Lucy wouldn't let him into her bedroom.

'Ah, hello,' said Tom, coming out of his dressing-room in shirt and trousers.

'I'm afraid I'm early.'

'Find yourself a drink. Good. Good.' Tom disappeared again.

Alex wandered down into the drawing-room, which was filled with the sweet smell of white jasmine, and then decided he wasn't ready for a drink.

'Oh, hi!' Eliza put her head round the door. 'I thought it might be you.''

Alex flung himself into the sofa. 'Keep me company. I'm far too early.'

'You are rather. Would you like a drink?'

'Everyone keeps offering me a drink. Do I look like a drunkard?'

'Well, I can't stay long.' Eliza sat down demurely beside him. 'Jessica's here.'

'Shall Mohammed come to the mountain, then?'

'Oh, no.'

'Whatever are you up to?'

Eliza blushed and looked away. 'Nothing really. Well, actually, we're going to make ourselves up. I'm just going up to borrow some stuff from Mummy.'

'Isn't your mother's beauty all nature's own?'

'Oh, yes. But . . .'

'But?'

'I must go really.'

'All right, but I'll visit you later. Look over the painted women.'

'Bring us some peppermint chocs. Those little thin ones from the table. Mummy never lets us have them usually.'

'Anything to make me welcome.'

*

Tom sat at one end of the large dining-table and gazed at his wife. Chloe, who was on his left, saw where he was looking and smiled. There was no use trying to start a conversation with Tom when he was looking at Lucy; not even about her since Tom never spoke about his wife to anyone. Further down the table, Alex was also looking at Lucy. His glance was quick and vindictive. Lucy herself was enthralled by Darrell's conversation. He was seated on her left.

'Colour sense is inborn. We ruin it by constant contact with the mediocre.'

'Babies only like red.' Lucy picked up a scarlet strawberry between her white fingers and popped it into her pink mouth.

'Babies?' repeated Darrell, losing his train of thought.

Alex shook the silver sugar castor vigorously over his plate. He had not been pacified by the young and pretty girl whom Lucy had made his neighbour. Putting down the castor he turned to her intensely,

'It was all a question of the length of the knife. If it had been a millimetre shorter it would have missed a main artery, merely severing a minor vein which would have caused severe haemorrhaging instead of loss of life.'

'I see,' the girl quivered with both fear and excitement at his strange onslaught. She had only asked him about his work in the politest sense.

Alex fixed his shining eyes on her low neckline and taking a pearl-handled knife from the table, waved it slowly in front of her bosom. She leant back nervously.

'Oh, dear,' said Chloe who couldn't help seeing her brother's odd behaviour. Tom looked too. And so did Lucy. She rose to her feet and the ladies, like moving flowers, gathered around her. Gracefully, they swished from the room.

Left to his own devices, Alex raised the knife in his hand and looked intently along the blade. It flew out of his hand.

'Bravo!' cried Tom.

'Not bad.' Smiling, Alex leant across and recovered the knife. Speared on its silver blade were three peppermint creams. 'Not bad for one throw.'

*

Eliza and Jessica were having a wonderful time; their faces already looked like an artist's palette and they hadn't finished yet.

'Do you think more white on my cheekbones?' Eliza peered into her little dressing-table mirror.

'More brown underneath, I think.' Jessica looked up consideringly from the floor. They had quite lost track of the time. There was a knock at the door.

'May I come in?' Alex stood swayingly. Now that he had left the support of the dining-room table, he appeared quite drunk.

Eliza's head swivelled round. She had tied back her dark hair. Her eyes, around which she had painted long black eyelashes, seemed huge and blue; her mouth for which she had chosen a raspberry pink glistened invitingly; her cheeks painted with shadows had lost their childish roundness. Alex stared. He thought he was seeing Lucy.

'Hip. Hip. Here's Alex with our chocs,' Eliza's voice rang out in girlish contradiction to her face. Silently Alex handed over the sweets. Eliza took them seriously and prepared to give one to Jessica.

'No, thank you. I'm not hungry.' Jessica lifted her sharp chin to watch Alex. 'Besides, there's a hole through them.'

'What?' Eliza looked down. 'So there is. Did you start eating them, Alex?'

'Don't be silly. He wouldn't do that.'

Alex recovered himself, 'I stabbed them,' he touched Eliza's darkened cheek, 'specially for you.'

'That's stupid.' Jessica stood up jealously.

'Thank you, Alex. It's a real mint with a hole,' Eliza smiled and putting the chocolate in her mouth began to suck happily.

Alex came right into the room and sat down heavily upon the bed.

'Aren't you going back to the party?' asked Eliza. 'Mummy'll miss you.'

'No, she won't. She's having a marvellous time.'

'But she always does. She's a great enjoyer. She believes it's sinful to be dreary and gloomy when you've got no reason.'

'What if you have a reason?'

'Oh, well. She hates people who are all pale and wishy-washy and droop about with hang-dog expressions. She doesn't see the point of having them around. She thinks they should stay out of sight till they feel ready for company again.'

'Wherever did you get all this?'

Eliza was embarrassed. She caught sight of Jessica's mocking eyes and fell silent. Jessica answered for her,

'She's always thinking about her mother.'

'No, I'm not.'

Alex turned to Jessica, 'What do *you* think about?'

Eliza saw the opportunity to get her own back,

'Boys!' she cried. 'She only thinks of boys. Which I think's pretty boring. Boys! Boys! Boys!'

*

The day after the dinner party was Sunday. A day which always received a special family formula. First of all there was Mass.

The priest, standing high on the altar, raised the golden glinting chalice. Lucy's face lifted and then sank again. Her eyes closed, the darkened lashes lying gently on her smooth cheeks, her pink lips murmured, 'My lord and my God.' Beside her Tom also bowed his head, though his was more of a military inclination, and beside him Rupert ducked his head in imitation while Eliza next along the line dropped her head so steeply that her hair swept across her face. Ticky, holding her mother's left hand, shook her head about enthusiastically.

Behind them various members of the congregation thought that there was no sight more beautiful than a Catholic family united in their communion with God. It made sense of life.

Lucy prayed. And her prayer was fervent for her family and those she loved. She prayed with the conviction or the faith that she would be answered. For who is not a sinner?

*

In the Trevelyans' house Jessica who had stayed overnight was whiling away the time until they returned. She tried on several of Eliza's clothes which she particularly coveted and then, running out of further ideas, sat down at the mirror to look for good points in her face. She had always found her combination of brown eyes, brown hair and sallow skin an unenlivening prospect, and since the make-up from the night before was still littered around, it was quite natural to try further experiments.

She didn't hear the doorbell ring. Maria let Alex in.

'They're all at church, sir.'

'I know. I know. I'll wait.'

'Miss Jessica's waiting downstairs, sir. Will you be here at lunch, sir?'

'I don't know.'

Irritated by all Maria's remarks, Alex went into the drawing-room. How dare Lucy find comfort and satisfaction at church while he wandered the streets, a lost soul, lusting for her body! Nervously, he drew out a big photograph album from under one of the pretty inlaid tables. At least he could look at her.

*

At church, the Trevelyan family was going up to the altar rails to take communion. Even Lucy received the holy wafer because she believed with the modern school that it should be taken by the weak wishing to be made strong, as well as by the already virtuous. 'Body of Christ.' 'Amen.'

'Body of Christ.' 'Amen.' Once more their heads were bowed in a row along the bench.

*

Alex, opening the album at the beginning, had found a smiling picture of Harald, his predecessor in Lucy's affections. Although he moved on quickly to where his own face appeared amidst jovial, mostly Scottish, family scenes, the image rankled. However, he might have been mollified by a half-page close-up of himself, had not a loose newspaper clipping fluttered out of the end pages. It showed Lucy and Darrell attending his production of *A Midsummer Night's Dream*. Her face was lifted towards his and one of her most glorious closed-lipped but sensuously inviting smiles was directed towards him. In it Alex saw her plan for the future and for his own dismissal. He looked furiously round the bright room filled with sunshine and its gay serenity was only a reflection of Lucy. A sudden urge to destroy took hold of him. He might have smashed her knick-knacks, torn down her pictures, hacked her creamy curtains, kicked at the prettily burning fire. Instead, he shut the book loudly and, letting it fall to the floor, went quickly from the room.

Jessica started guiltily when the bedroom door opened, for she was still wearing Eliza's dress.

'Oh, it's you.' She sounded relieved.

Alex shut the door carefully behind him and went over to Jessica. He registered that her face wore the same bright colours which in Eliza had reminded him of Lucy. He was glad, for it made his task more pleasurable.

'They are being a long time,' said Jessica more shyly, now she had him to herself. 'Have you been here long?'

Alex didn't answer her, but lifting up her long hair unzipped the dress.

'Oh, be careful, it's Eliza's,' said Jessica rather wildly.

His action had caused such a reaction in her of terror and delight that she could do nothing. Alex smiled grimly. Her daughter's dress too. He made Jessica step out of it carefully and then folded it over a chair. The perfect justice of the step he was about to take satisfied his lawyer's mind. It was obviously pre-ordained, inevitable.

'What are you doing?' said Jessica weakly, as he pushed her onto the bed. It was like her wildest imaginings.

'Sssshhhh.' Alex took off his trousers. Jessica watched mesmerized and all sorts of thoughts raced through her mind. She put one arm behind her head and as she did so caught sight of a large poster of Marc Bolan above the bed. Fear gave way to a bold exhilaration of what was about to happen. Yet one part of her mind remained cool enough to think how this would cancel out all Eliza's superiority. Eliza might be prettier, cleverer, richer. But she, Jessica, would have Alex. How it would shock her ... though she would never tell ... it would be her own secret. Her ...

'Ah,' Jessica gasped, as Alex's full weight descended on her. Her thoughts slid away under a renewal of fear, but by now it was too late to cry out or draw back.

'Vengeance,' thought Alex in a kind of madness. And although he had only looked to stop his suffering, he found a sort of mindless enjoyment in this sex without love.

*

The congregation knelt as the priest turned to face them. 'Go in peace,' he said. 'The Mass is ended.'

Rupert and Ticky burst out of the church and ran gaily along the pavement mottled with sunlight. Eliza took Tom's arm who was following more slowly.

'I loved the sermon. That bit about the blood of the lamb turning to Coca-Cola.'

'Eliza. How could you!' Lucy seemed upset out of all

proportion. 'Priests shouldn't lower themselves to that sort of talk. Such a vulgar modern thing to say. The Church should bring an image of beauty and purity into our lives, not ugliness.'

'Well, I thought it quite telling.'

Tom laughed. He squeezed Eliza's arm. 'What odd words you use. Your mother's quite right of course – fundamentally. But you'd get many more people to agree with you.'

'That's me. Out on a limb.' Lucy spoke lightly.

'You're a product of the eighteenth century.'

'What does that mean?' Eliza skipped round to face them.

'It means you've got a beautiful mother.'

'I know that.' Their conversation had brought them to a gate to Hampstead Heath through which they often returned to the house.

'Ah!' Lucy began to run. Like a young girl, she chased among the russet-coloured leaves.

'Wait for me!' cried Eliza.

'Mummy, Mummy!' called Rupert and Ticky.

Tom watched; and mother and children looked to him the same elfin size, whirling and dancing in a joyous pattern. The sight both filled him with love and also with a dread of the fragility of their happiness. He said a prayer for them all. He would have given up his life to protect them.

*

The note was scrawled in lipstick on Eliza's mirror. 'Gone home. You-know-what started. See you.'

'How odd,' thought Eliza. 'I'm sure it was only two weeks ago. Oh, well.'

She flung herself on the bed and retrieved *Anna Karenina* from under the pillow. That would have to amuse her till lunch. Rather annoyed, she noticed several of the pages had got scrumpled. She smoothed them lovingly.

*

Alex was reading the Sunday papers in the drawing-room.

'Oh,' said Lucy coming upon him suddenly. Her face was cold. Alex smiled.

'It was such a particularly beautiful morning that only a particularly beautiful woman would do.'

'Oh.'

But Alex was quite undeterred by this lack of enthusiasm, 'You look like the morning, sparkling, young, fresh and pure.' And as this still provoked no response from Lucy, he continued on another tack. 'Do you know London's air pollution ratio has fallen by 5 per cent? Tom will be pleased.' And then apparently unable to contain his confident good spirits, he gave her a brazen look over the newspaper. 'You don't mind me coming, do you?' He seemed convinced the question was purely rhetorical. 'I'm feeling so entertaining today. Your lunch table would be quite drab without me.'

Lucy wavered. She could never resist self-confidence. Alex, with his smiling handsome face and air of self-congratulation, was all she most liked in a male.

Tom came into the room, 'Uh. Good. Staying to lunch?'

'If your wife relents. Do you know London's air pollution ...?'

'Good. Good.'

Lucy, who was dressed mostly in cream, chose a mulberry-coloured chair and curled up her long legs. She stretched forward for a newspaper and then hesitated a moment. She looked at Alex who returned her look with unblinking eyes. His whites looked particularly white. Her lips curled involuntarily and she forgot to wonder what had changed the sulky schoolboy of the night before into this charming social animal.

'You'll have to play me at back-gammon,' she smiled at him challengingly, 'and I warn you, I'm in holy conquering form.'

'It'll be my pleasure,' Alex leant forward eagerly, 'but I assure you, I'm on pretty good form myself.'

'The battle's on then,' cried Lucy with a trilling excited laugh.

'Arrhum.' Tom apparently deep in his newspaper cleared his throat.

4

Lucy sat on the swing seat in her garden. Although it was late autumn, almost winter, her pretty white barrels and curly stone urns still overflowed with greenery. Only the young chestnut tree above her head gave way to the seasons, with a last graceful scattering of leaves that floated round her head like paper birds before descending.

'I don't want you to look sad. It's so dismal looking at unsmiling faces, don't you think?' Chloe was crouching in front of Lucy. She held a grotesquely large black camera.

'But I'm not sad.' Lucy, without moving from her pose, legs draped along the seat, one hand raised to support her face, expressed surprise. 'In fact I was thinking quite the opposite.' A small breeze blew a curl across her face. 'Would you . . . ?' A young boy flashed from behind Chloe to smooth it back, sprayed just a touch of lacquer and disappeared once more.

'I was thinking how well everything was going,' resumed Lucy. 'The *Akropolis* is my biggest job ever. Real money for once. Do you know I'm the first woman ever to decorate a liner? They'll enrol me in Women's Lib, if I'm not careful.' Lucy laughed.

'Yes. But you mustn't talk,' said Chloe, looking down her camera. 'Unless we do natural-type pictures, and the mag doesn't like that.' Lucy replied by smiling sweetly and Chloe, without taking her eyes from her, handed her empty camera to a youth at her shoulder. She received another without turning.

'You'll just have to listen to me. Not that I've much to say. My darling Martin's promised to leave his wife again, but that's hardly news. Except – perhaps, I'm worried about Alex.'

Lucy's eyes opened wide and Chloe captured the look of astonishment, though she knew it would not be flattering enough to pass Lucy's blue pencil. 'Yes. He's odd. He's got the same sort of look as when he spiked my goldfish. He was always very intense underneath. I know he seems so smooth and charming but that's mostly a public-school veneer. Once he gets a bee in his bonnet, he'll stick with it through everything. I'll never forget his rages as a boy; they terrified me. His eyes went glassy green and he'd stare at a point about my navel level as if he wanted to knife it. Once he came at me with a twelve bore . . .'

This was too much for Lucy,

'Oh, Chloe, really . . .' she smiled disbelievingly.

'Sshh.' Chloe wagged her finger magisterially. 'I must say, it's fun having a captive audience. All right, I'm not saying he's coming at anyone with a gun, but he is behaving strangely. He's avoiding me for one thing, which is quite unusual as I'm the only person he can talk to about you.' Chloe paused, for Lucy's photographic smile had at her last words become even more rigidly beatific. Chloe remembered she did not like the idea of Alex talking about her to any-one, even his sister – least of all his sister. 'You look a bit stiff,' she suggested not very tactfully. 'Let's have a change round.'

'But Alex's been so much the conquering hero lately,' Lucy relaxed her legs and took her face off her hand. 'Quite his old self. A joy to us all. No forcing himself forward, but always ready to amuse. And Tom say's he's been *épouvantable* at the Bar.'

'Oh, well,' Chloe stroked her camera lovingly, for in

truth she was more interested at the moment in taking good photographs than in her brother, 'Now, I want a giant close-up.'

'Oh, Chloe. In daylight. At my age,' Lucy protested not very convincingly. She settled her face into lines of disciplined happiness. For she knew happiness rampant was not very photogenic. And she was happy.

*

Eliza was wandering back from school. Once again Jessica had disappeared before she could suggest they walked home together. It was beginning to look as if she was avoiding her purposefully and yet she couldn't think of any reason for that. Perhaps she had B.O. Smiling, she swung her case into the air and broke into a determined jog-trot.

*

'Why do you always leave your hat on till last?'

'Because I like it best.' Jessica snapped up the elastic of her school panama and pulled it off her head.

'Throw it here,' Alex leant out of bed to catch it. 'But it's horribly unfashionable. You look much better without it.' He put out a hand towards her naked body. Jessica allowed herself to be pulled into the bed. Alex looked for a moment past her to her school uniform folded over the chair. It was the same chair that bore the luxurious swathes of Lucy's discarded clothes. Alex smiled. It was not a vindictive smile, but a smile in sheer enjoyment at the contrast between his two mistresses. If you could elevate Jessica to the stature of a mistress. And yet in some ways she was as hardbitten as an old whore. For instance she didn't seem at all worried by her anomalous position – probably, Alex thought, understanding more of the implications than she let on. He couldn't think why Eliza had chosen her for a friend or why Lucy had allowed such an unbeautiful person into the house.

'You don't seem as young as . . .' He started before deciding such comparisons were odious and too near reality for his relationship with Jessica.

'I'm not as young as her,' said Jessica, who was quick about things like this. 'She's fourteen and I'm nearly sixteen. We were just in the same class because I'm not so clever as her. I'm only ten years younger than you. That's not much.'

'Oh, it is.' Almost absentmindedly Alex ran his hand over her breasts.

'It's all ten years, isn't it? I'm ten years younger than you and you're ten years younger than . . . Owwhh! You pinched me!'

Alex rolled lazily over until his body covered hers, there was one name he didn't want to hear on her lips.

'Little girls should be seen and not heard.'

*

Lucy was smiling at Alex across the table. She had meant it to be a quick lunch, snatched between fantastic swirls of silk for the liner's curtains. But instead here they were, in their own special restaurant, nearly three o'clock and still lingering over their coffee.

'I wear your favour in my helmet like a medieval knight.'

'Don't other maidens try and snatch it out?'

'Impossible. It's stuck with a magic glue.'

Lucy giggled, 'We sound like a commercial for Bostik. What does my favour look like?'

'Pink. Gossamer in appearance but steel in texture. It

tinkles when the wind blows. Like a bell round a goat's neck.'

'Oh, no. They're hideous.'

'I take that as a compliment.'

'You may.'

'Lucy?'

'Yes.' She cast her eyes down mysteriously.

'I've no case this afternoon.'

'What? Can it be the knight wants to remove his lady from her pedestal? Take heed, it may be dangerous.'

''Tis true; but I have a special potion that shall preserve me.'

'Then let us away,' said Lucy, eyes shining into his.

'In all haste.' Alex waved at the waiter and a warm glow of sexual anticipation, untainted by any mean jealousies, spread through him. He half-smiled at the thought of common little Jessica as a special potion; and yet it was quite true. She had immunized him against Lucy's superiority. Lucy had her husband and her children and her household. He had her daughter's friend as a lover.

Lucy took her fur coat from the waiter, who was always so flatteringly attentive, with a delicious sense of expectation. Although she chose only partly to analyse her choice and changes from lover to lover she was aware that the silver scale which a week or two ago had been tipping in Darrell's masterful direction was now returning to Alex's more civilized appeal. He adored her so. He was so amusing, such a success at his job, so sought after in society and yet so utterly devoted! Darrell's devotion, she realized, was not quite so complete, even if his respect for her work was greater. She pulled the coat round her so that the soft fur stroked her hot cheek. Ah, how glorious it was to be slightly tipsy and on the way to afternoon love!

They walked out of the restaurant into air that had become, with the approaching winter, sharp and cold and Alex felt quite free and independent. Only the glow that filled his body drew him to Lucy. He hailed a taxi.

*

'Why do you keep running away from me?' Eliza had at last managed to pin down Jessica as the morning's lessons finished. They stood by the door to the classroom watching the other girls filing out to lunch.

'I don't.'

'That's silly. You haven't come home for nearly two weeks and you used to come every other day.'

'I'm busy.' Jessica tried to move into the corridor. Eliza, with the determination of her mother, blocked her way.

'I'll only let you go if you sit next to me at lunch.'

'If you must be so childish.' Disdainfully, Jessica gave in.

When they had filled their plates with liver and onion, Eliza attacked again.

'Do I have B.O. or something? Honestly, it's enough to give a girl a complex.'

'Don't be so childish.'

'Why do you keep saying I'm childish?'

'Well, I'm older than you.' Jessica poked at her liver with distaste.

'You always have been.'

'It shows more now. Anyway, I'm going to leave school.'

'Jessica! You can't. Our exams. We were going to swot up together. You can't do anything without exams.'

'This liver's revolting. It makes me feel quite sick.'

Eliza looked at her interestedly. 'You do look rather green,' she giggled. 'Is it because Miss Mata said the Elizabethans thought the liver was the seat of the passions ... Jessie! Where you are going?'

But she was too late. Fist stuffed in her mouth, Jessica was making a very fast exit from the dining-room.

'Oh.' Rather dazedly, Eliza surveyed the empty place and the full plate and then absentmindedly, she prodded her fork into a piece of Jessica's untouched liver. Actually, it was jolly good.

*

Lucy was attending a nursery tea. She wasn't eating because she wasn't in that sort of mood. She was rather gracing a function with her presence. She had worked hard all day, seeing no one and her head, filled for hours with colours and shapes, with sofas and chairs, carpeting and candelabra, was gradually turning to the prospect of a well-earned evening out with, for a change, Tom as her escort. Even that, in her mood of virtuous fulfilment, pleased her. Tom could be more entertaining than anyone, when the situation was right. And it would be tonight. The children, with their own adventures of the day, were so lively and gay that, although on their own they could not have created her mood, they now added to her conviction that it was a perfectly delightful day.

'And did the fairy baby kiss you, darling?' she encouraged the sweetly romancing Ticky.

'Oh, yeth. Over and over.'

*

Jessica's mother, Mrs Byrd, had only just pressed the doorbell to the Trevelyan house, when Eliza joined her on the doorstep.

'Oh, hello, Mrs Byrd,' she called out blithely. 'Whatever's the matter with Jessica these days? She won't have anything to do . . .'

'I've come to see your mother,' Mrs Byrd interrupted her brusquely. She had a lot to be brusque about, for she was square and unattractive, untalented and generally unfavoured by the gods. Her husband had left her when Jessica was nine. She had been flattered by her daughter's friendship with the daughter of such a fashionable, clever, successful family. Now she would take her revenge for their patronage.

'I expect she's up in the nursery. Do come in and I'll take you up.'

Mrs Byrd was further annoyed by Eliza's beautiful manners and strode up the stairs with a darker scowl than ever.

She knew exactly what she was going to say, having rehearsed it all the way to the house, but nevertheless she was greatly put off by Lucy's appearance. She sat among her children looking as young and innocent as her own daughter.

'Darling!' she welcomed, at first only seeing Eliza and pleased to have her whole clutch about her.

'I've brought Mrs Byrd up,' said Eliza. 'She was on the doorstep.'

'I've come to see you,' said Mrs Byrd in tones that should have sounded foreboding, but instead seemed rather silly.

'Of course.' Lucy was pleased to have another potential admirer. 'Won't you have a cup of tea?'

'Alone,' enunciated Mrs Byrd, partly recovering her dignity.

Lucy was only slightly startled and jumped up gaily from her seat. 'I do see your point. They are rather a brood. Let's go downstairs to the drawing-room.'

The door had barely closed on them before Mrs Byrd burst her banks of wrath,

'Whore!' she shouted. 'Whore!'

Lucy, curled elegantly in the sofa, seemed to shrivel at the word. It was as if she had waited for it all her life. The Emperor's New Clothes. All her social lustre and commanding confidence disappeared into shocked passivity. She could make no sound. No defence.

So Mrs Byrd had her rampage. It was a debauch for her. She became flushed and her eyes glazed. She would have been a revolting sight were it not that she had justice on her side. Lucy's lover had seduced Lucy's daughter's best friend. On a Sunday. While they were at church. And now the girl was pregnant. She stood over Lucy, arms flailing, and reached her revolting climax. 'It could have been your daughter!'

At last Lucy was galvanized into a response. She stared up at this ugly demon who had come to ruin her beautiful life with horror.

'What do you want? Why have you come here? What can I do?'

Mrs Byrd went on remorselessly, 'She was under age, you know. Not yet sixteen; legally under age. He'd know all about that, of course, her seducer being a lawyer himself.'

Lucy would normally have smiled at such a melodramatic word, but in this case she trembled, 'Her seducer.'

'And your . . .' Mrs Byrd paused and looked at Lucy in insolent insinuation but then seemed to change her mind. 'Your husband's a Queen's Counsellor,' she said. 'What will his colleagues think of a scandal . . .?'

'We'll do anything we can to help,' murmured Lucy.

*

Lucy burst into tears when she saw Tom. He looked so firm and comforting. She very seldom cried unless it was with passion, so Tom at once put his arm round her anxiously. They sat down together on a sofa in the drawing-room and Lucy cast about how to begin telling her husband the sordid tale. She shuddered at the words she would have to use and thanked God that at least she could rely on him to understand with the minimum of explanations.

In fact he stayed calm throughout. 'Eliza must never know,' he said at length.

'No. No. That would be dreadful. At her age. So delicate. Half child half woman. And she worships Alex. She absolutely mustn't. Whatever happens, Eliza must never know. She wouldn't understand anything. She's too young.' Lucy heard herself rising to hysteria and subsided, ashamed.

'Will she take money?' Tom asked quietly.

'I don't know. She didn't directly say. She seemed to want to make me writhe. She was so ugly . . . Yes, I expect she'll take money.' Lucy paused and reflected. 'Alex hasn't any money. Not enough.' She hesitated again.

'Don't worry,' said Tom.

There was a pause, a silence and then Lucy spoke heatedly again.

'I'll never have him in the house. I'll never see him. He's a destroyer. I thought he was something bright and creative and . . . a good force. But he's not. He's twisted. He came into the middle of our happy family and . . .'

'I think you should get changed for dinner,' Tom interrupted her gently.

'Oh!' Lucy looked dazed and then slightly relieved; without saying any more she rose obediently. But when she was standing, she seemed like a marionette, to be waiting for someone to pull the strings.

'Don't worry,' said Tom again, without moving from his fireside chair and his tone held no bitterness or reproach, 'Forget about it. Alex is a reasonable man but he's young. People do things they regret when they're young.' Lucy still stood unmoving. 'You won't see him again. Jessica won't see him again. Chloe and I will smooth it over.'

'Chloe?' said Lucy dubiously as if wondering

whether the sister of such a man could still be her friend.

'I want you to wear that green dress we got in Paris,' said Tom.

'Ah.' Lucy stirred as if the green dress had produced a vision. She walked briskly from the room. In fact her vision had been of the last time she had worn it which had happened to be with Darrell. For a flash she had seen with a queer relief his hard almost brutal face. There would be no insinuating surprises from him. She thanked God for a husband like Tom. And yet already she was taking for granted his power to banish her nightmares. Why else had she married a man like him; a man so much older than herself?

Tom sat in the drawing-room and his face looked grey and old. It seemed that Lucy had drained from him all his strength. Moving stiffly he went to the drinks table and poured himself a large whisky. He took it with him to the mantelpiece where he leant heavily. The size of the drink reminded him of Scotland where it was taken as a remedy against the freezing powers of the loch; there, they had been happy – he allowed himself to picture rosy cheeks in laughing faces, dark trees against blue skies – then as the warmth from the fire began to spread through his body, he faced what he must do for Lucy, for his family, for himself. The look of determination made him once more the man upon whom Lucy relied.

At that moment the door was flung open and Eliza came bouncing in.

'Hello, Daddy.' She gave him a perky kiss. Tom received it as a confirmation of his decision. Eliza stood back and surveyed him critically.

'You'd better hurry up and change. Mummy's nearly ready and she looks superbly beautiful.'

With a start of surprise Tom heard the small gilded clock on the mantelpiece strike eight. He looked at his watch unbelievingly. Lucy had left him an hour ago. He put out a hand to Eliza's hair and then stretched his back which had stiffened as he stood.

'You're quite right, my darling. Lucky you came and found me.'

'Will you wear that wide purpley tie I especially like?' Eliza asked eagerly.

'Anything to please a lady.' Tom paused, half-turned his face from his daughter's. 'Do you see much of that friend of yours,' with an effort he pronounced her name, 'Jessica, these days?'

Eliza negligently studied a strand of her hair, 'Well, she's still at school.'

'I see.'

'But I don't like her much any more,' she continued in a rush of confidence. 'At least to start with she went off me but now I think she's stuck up and silly. And stupid too!' She ended with a malicious flourish.

'She is a bit different from you, I think.' Tom was still wary. 'People do often drift apart. So you won't worry too much if she – she leaves school?'

'Oh, no! Heavens no! Honestly she's not worth talking about!' Eliza flung back her head defiantly and then gave her father a half shove in the back. 'But do hurry up. You'll be so late. And you know how Mummy hates to wait.'

Obediently Tom left the room. His face had lightened a fraction. Perhaps it would all work out.

*

Alex's affaire with Jessica, which had started in anger as a desperate measure of self-defence, had soon become an essential part of his life. Guilt-free in regard to Jessica because she was so unlike an innocent school girl and in regard to Lucy because he was so convinced of the justice of his action, he never considered the possibility of discovery. If he had, he might have also thought of the harm his action could do to the innocent – to Lucy's family, her daughter, her husband. But Lucy's dominant personality had always obscured a proper view of her children or Tom.

All Alex knew was that he had found a way of continuing sane and remaining in Lucy's favour. He did not consider that what he thought was sanity might appear dangerous madness to anyone else.

It was nine o'clock in the morning when Tom summoned Alex to his office. As they were in the same chambers this only meant bounding up a couple of flights of stairs.

Tom had already come to an agreement with Jessica's mother – a transaction which had offended against all his principles. Now he only wanted to deal with Alex as quickly as possible. Coldly he told him that he had been found out. Brusquely he gave him an ultimatum. Lucy's name was never mentioned.

Alex was too stunned to make any answer to Tom. He too could not bear to mention Lucy's name to her husband. He sat in white-faced silence.

Tom said slowly and clearly,

'If you make any attempt to see Jessica or anyone in my house ever again, I shall have you dismissed from chambers.' It would not be difficult for Tom as head of chambers and the man who had originally introduced Alex into the chambers to carry out this threat.

At last the reality of the situation seemed to dawn on Alex. He jumped to his feet,

'You can't blackmail me. I'm not a criminal . . .'

'You are,' Tom spoke wearily. 'She's under sixteen.'

Alex sat down again. None of this was to the point. The whole Jessica business was altogether beside the point. Jessica had only been a paltry means to an end. A nothing.

Lucy was the point. The point of his life. But he could never now say Lucy's name to her husband. He saw that the step which had seemed the only way to draw him closer to Lucy would be the cause of their total separation. She would never look at him now. What did it matter about his job; about anything, if he could not see Lucy?

Tom would not allow himself to feel pity for the man slumped in front of him. He let the vision of Lucy's glowing beauty, of Eliza's childlike innocence blot out his face.

'You agree?'

Alex looked at him vacantly and then since nothing mattered any more and he needed desperately to be alone, he said, 'Yes. Yes. Whatever you say. I . . .' He got up again and, staggering slightly, left the room. He thought he might be sick.

Tom picked up his Biro and began to scribble on his blotter. Without being conscious of what he was doing, he wrote Lucy's name several times and finally picked up the telephone.

'Would you get Mrs Trevelyan please?' He waited impatiently to hear her soft voice. Lucy reserved a special helpless voice for the telephone's sharp interruption. As if she'd been surprised from some reverie.

'Tom, darling.' Lucy picked up the phone in her office; as soon as she heard his voice she knew without asking that the matter was settled. She felt as if her heartbeat became quicker, gayer, as if her whole body had suddenly become lighter, brighter. She looked out of the window and sunbeams were dancing through the glass.

'Oh, darling!' And in her gratitude she was about to suggest they lunched together, until she remembered she had already promised Darrell. 'It's such a beautiful day!'

*

Nevertheless, in the days that followed, Lucy's restored happiness was marred by a lingering worry.

'Mummy,' Eliza said in her serious girlish way. 'Whatever's happened to Alex? I haven't seen him for ages.'

Lucy, although she lay in a warm scented bath, felt herself turn cold. What could she say to Eliza? She could not, would not tell lies – that had never been her way – but then what explanation could she make?

'Oh, I expect he's been busy,' she replied lightly, despising her cowardice. 'We'll ask Chloe.' She stood up rather less gracefully than usual, 'Pass the towel, would you, darling.'

But once having mentioned Chloe's name the idea that she could help took hold of her. At the same time she admitted to herself that Tom's delicacy in not telling her how he had settled the horror had at first absolved her of all fear, but lately had left her nervously doubtful that Alex had disappeared forever. She, more than Tom, knew the strength of his love for her.

So she decided she must talk to Chloe.

*

Chloe was photographing one of Lucy's bathrooms when Lucy found her, and she immediately became so much part of her camera that only Lucy's iron determination still looked for sympathy or advice. Chloe stood on the marble-topped table with her giant eye fixed on the large brass taps. Lucy, defiantly dressed in scarlet, held the camera case.

'The point is Eliza. She adores him. What can I tell her? I've absolutely racked my brains and can only think of silly things, like he's got married which she'd absolutely never believe. Really it's worrying me haggard!'

Chloe looked ironically at Lucy's glowing face and stepped down onto the lavatory seat,

'I warned you,' she said unhelpfully.

'Darling Chloe. I know you did. I'm not blaming you.' The lightness of her tone sounded brittle. 'You can't help having a destroyer for a brother.' She paused, struck afresh by the fact of Chloe being sister to such a monster, then continued nevertheless, 'But you're so good at solutions. I think it's spending so much time watching the world from behind that camera of yours.'

'Tell her he's gone to America.'

'Why ever should she believe that?'

'Because it's true. He's thrown up the Bar and gone to New York. So you're quite safe, you see.'

'Oh,' gasped Lucy, overlooking the sharp tone of Chloe's last remark. 'Gone. For how long?'

'There's nothing for him here now.'

'No.' A feeling of relief began in Lucy.

'He wants to get away from it all. Start a new life. I shouldn't think he'll come back for ages. It was a kind of madness.' Chloe paused and then said slowly, 'I think he knows that now.'

'Yes,' agreed Lucy but she wasn't really listening. Now she knew Alex was safely out of the way, she had no reason ever to think of him again. He had killed all happy recollections of their glorious romantic times together. For her, he was dead.

'Thank God, then,' she exclaimed. After all that she had suffered it was as if a thunder cloud had sailed away, revealing the brilliant blue sky behind. Now she could look Eliza in the face again and give her an honest explanation of Alex's non-appearance which she would never question. Now she would shake her head clear of the mists and darkness and look only to the light.

She began in her mind to plan the beautiful Christmas they would have in Scotland. Her happy innocent children, Chloe, Darrell . . .

'Chloe, you will come for Christmas, won't you?' she cried impulsively.

Chloe climbed off the table where she had been standing throughout their conversation and, as she came face to face with Lucy, was struck anew by her serene and youthful beauty. No pain or guilt blurred its edges. It had not occurred to Lucy that Chloe might blame her for ruining her brother's life. And she was right; Chloe put her camera carefully on the table; she could never criticize Lucy. She admired her too much. To be completely honest – and Chloe never hesitated from an honest view of herself – she would like to behave exactly as Lucy did. She suspected most women would,

'Of course I'll come. You know I adore Scotland.' But of course Lucy would always be unique. Perhaps it was just as well.

Now Lucy's relief had made her light-headed,

'You must have finished, Chloe! Let's have lunch. Let's have a disgustingly greedy, wildly expensive lunch at Tiberio and then go shopping or at least window-shopping down Bond Street, take in a few galleries and then see who we can find from Sotheby's for tea in Claridges . . . and then . . . !'

Chloe was an easy victim for such enthusiasm.

*

Lucy was proved right about the way Eliza would accept the news of Alex's departure. Although piqued that he had not wished her good-bye, she never thought of asking why he had gone. He was still separated from this sort of question by the barrier between child and adult. However her conviction that he was the most perfect example of manhood remained firm, and if anything was increased by his removal from her life at an age when she was still capable of uncritical adoration. Secretly – because she sensed hero-worship was a childish occupation – she thought of him often. And on evenings when she was alone in the drawing-room, she would turn the pages of the same photograph album that had so annoyed Alex himself, and sigh over his picture.

Darrell, though now as keen to win her approval as Alex had ever been, had come too late to compete. Besides, she was still hooked on long aristocratic legs.

INTERMISSION

*

Nearly two years passed. Lucy changed her lover for a newer, younger, more adaptable model. Tom worked and watched over his family. Eliza grew up from child to woman. And Alex returned to London.

It was a peaceful time.

5

Alex's departure was followed by Christmas. Christmas was
followed by work. It was with relief that Lucy became the
interior decorator again. Although she could never pretend
to find anonymity through her work, it took her away from
her London home at a time when it had become a little
sullied, a little less than beautiful. Besides, the Greek liner
on which she now started to work full time was turning
out to be a complicated and absorbing challenge for her
talents. The fear that her social reputation might mislead
people into thinking she was a dilettante had always
encouraged her to work harder than anyone. She had to be
respected as a professional. Darrell was helpful with this;
he gave her practical advice based on his own overlapping
experience as a stage designer and also, more important,
stimulated her self-respect with his serious attitude to her
career.

Lucy had always known, and been stimulated by the
knowledge that the quality of Tom's admiration would not
alter whether she lay in bed all day or became the first
woman to climb Everest.

'Beautiful, darling,' he would say, when she showed him a
design or an idea for a design. 'No one in London has such a
brilliant wife.'

Tom, himself, was conducting a long and complicated
case against a large oil-drilling company who had flooded
two miles of perfect coastline. Nevertheless, Lucy under-
estimated the added satisfaction he got from her success in
work. Certainly he could not love her more, but he could

feel a particular glow of security that she was happy and content. Darrell *in situ*, during the first of the two years, was a small price to pay. Tom dared to believe that his household was once more set fair for the future.

Eliza, also, was doing especially well at school and, to her own surprise, though not to her parents', had been put with a small group of cleverer girls who were to take their O Levels a year early, at fifteen.

'She's too bright for that school, really,' Lucy had said to Tom over dinner one evening. 'She's too big a fish in too small a pond.'

This thought had also occurred to Tom. It had prompted him into an idea for smoothing her way to maturity. He knew how a mother as perfect as Lucy could affect her. He looked at Lucy across the dinner table. She was idly sprinkling sugar onto a slice of pineapple. Her face looked relaxed, softer than usual.

'Perhaps she should find the world a bit?' he began casually. 'Leave school after her exams. Have a year in Paris. And then come back and take her A Levels from a crammers.'

Lucy was a little surprised that Tom should produce this plan apparently ready-made, but had to admit the sense of it. Besides, she had become aware lately that Eliza was entering that awkward stage of being too old for the nursery and yet not ready for the drawing-room. So Tom quietly effected a separation between mother and daughter.

Eliza herself felt that her relationship with her mother was not as easy as it had been. She could not worship at the altar of beauty and intelligence as unconsciously as she had before, although she had found nothing else in her present life to produce the same adoring emotion. Only the still-retained memory of Alex kept the same kind of hold over her imagination. She saw him once during those two years. One evening in early summer.

*

She had come in after school with an excited air.

'Lizzie? Is that you?' Her mother was calling from up-stairs. She started up.

'Look, darling,' Lucy came out of her bedroom; she flung a yellow cape round her shoulders, 'I'm just dashing to meet Darrell, he's found a marvellous new fabric printer. Would you mind wrapping the presents on my bed? Everything's there. For Rupert's birthday party. You know.'

'But Mummy, I wanted to ask you ... I wanted to go ...'

'Thank you so much, darling.' Lucy swept away.

Eliza entered the room resignedly and then rebelled. At least she would make her own arrangements first; unhook-ing the telephone receiver, she lay on the bed in the position she had seen her mother so often.

'Clare? Yes, I'm coming. Definitely. I tried to ask Mummy. But she didn't really listen ... She's very liberal about things anyway ...'

Clare was Jessica's replacement; a much more suitable friend, with blonde healthy looks and the sort of mind in-capable of surprises. She was a nice middle-class girl and as such a sensible foil for Eliza's special sharpness and beauty. Not that Eliza was quite beautiful yet, for although her eyes started brilliantly from her face there was something still in-decisively childish about her mouth and chin. She hadn't yet learned to project herself.

The two girls met in a wet cinema queue in Leicester Square. Above them shrieked a huge poster of a semi-nude girl. Blood poured from her mouth.

'Are you sure that review said it was a good film?' Eliza looked nervous.

'It said it was educational. That's the same thing.'

'The rain's taking off all my powder.'

'You're tall. You don't have to worry. They're sure to think you're eighteen.' Clare looked down at the excessively high pair of shoes she was wearing. 'I'll have to hang onto your arm.'

'I wish we were going to something else.' Eliza fingered the pearl earrings she'd taken from her mother's dressing-table as recompense for eventually wrapping Rupert's presents.

'Don't be such a spoil-sport. I tell you, it's had terrific reviews.' Clare paused and tottered closer. 'Do you know that man buying his ticket? He keeps peering round at you . . . Don't look now!'

But her warning was too late. Eliza stared straight into the smiling face of Alex.

'Alex!' she cried and then, suddenly remembering where she was, blushed a rosy pink. He came across to them immediately, leaving a young fair-haired girl by the box office. Without realizing what she was doing, Eliza gazed at her intensely. 'That's Clare.' Alex waved towards her and they all watched as the girl gracefully shook her yellow hair loose of her coat.

'So is this,' Eliza mumbled gauchely. And cast an agonized look at the sanguineous lady above their heads.

'That's easily done then.' Alex laughed.

'I didn't know you were back from America,' said Eliza almost accusingly.

'I'm not. At least, only for a few days.'

'Oh. I see.' Eliza looked again at the girl waiting for him. Her yellow hair and wide pink mouth reminded her of someone but she didn't identify it as her mother. 'You're not married, are you?' she said suddenly and once more blushed scarlet.

Alex laughed.

'Heavens no. What made you think that?'

'Well, I don't know.' Eliza, in confusion, and wanting to change the subject, found herself saying even more foolishly, 'You never said good-bye,' which she tried to hide by rushing on with, 'when do you go back – to America, I mean?'

'Tomorrow,' Alex looked out across the bright and noisy square, 'I'm working there. In Wall Street.'

'Oh, I see.' Eliza had only the vaguest idea of what Wall Street was. 'That's good.'

'It is. I'm making pots of money.'

'You look richer. Well. Different. Sort of bigger.'

'That sounds like an insult.'

'Oh, no, I mean,' thinking that she was appearing more childlike than ever, Eliza searched about for something about herself to impress him, 'I'm going to Paris for a year. After my exams.'

Alex waved his hand at the garish poster, 'Getting into practice, are you?' He paused and then added lightly, 'I'm surprised your mother lets you.'

Unaware of any change in Alex's tone Eliza began hurriedly,

'Oh, she doesn't kn –' before breaking off. She was quite relieved when the queue started to move.

'We'd better go on,' said Alex, 'but tell your mother I'll come back and take care of you, if she doesn't do a better job.' Alex and his Clare disappeared into the bright cinema.

'Who was he?' Clare whispered jealously. 'You seemed to know him awfully well.'

'Oh, just a friend of the family's.' Eliza was quite casual again. 'He used to stay a lot in Scotland. But then he went to New York. He's quite brilliant, of course.'

'I must say he's awfully good-looking. Oh, gosh! We're nearly at the doors. Smile, Eliza. Don't look as if you think we'll be turned away.'

Eliza's smile was so sweet to the doorman that he was quite dazzled and let in too many couples before putting up his hand.

Alex sat in the dark cinema and the film which he had chosen, as he chose most of his entertainment, for its escapist value, totally failed in its purpose. The threat of brutal sex, sadism, murder on the supposedly innocent bosoms that were being presented in such glorious Technicolor hardly kept his eyes occupied, let alone his mind. The meeting with Eliza, so totally unexpected and so out of place in the vulgar surroundings, had thrown him into confusion. He looked back with surprise at the trivial ease with which he had spoken to her. And about her mother. Lucy. He had prepared himself for a chance meeting with Lucy, but not with Eliza. He was left feeling disjointed; it had been like seeing a shadow of the real thing. All his emotions had been aroused by something that could not even give him the satisfaction of memory.

Love. Alex's life in America had not cured him of Lucy. But he had found New York a good place to suffer in – particularly for a personable bachelor. The wound had been anaesthetized by other girls, parties and, more recently, work. The job had arrived almost out of the blue. It was in the European division of an Investment Bank. He was surprised to find how easily he became a business man. Or to be more precise a 'Legal Consultant'. Within six months he was earning more than he had as a barrister in London, and he had lately begun to travel abroad for them. He had gathered in the course of interviews that someone who wished to remain anonymous had very highly recommended him and this was an important factor in his getting the job. Sometimes he wondered who his unknown benefactor was.

If his life was full, it was also unsettled. He moved by choice with a group of international ex-patriots who thought only in terms of the present. It suited him, because he still believed that his future would be with Lucy.

And now he had seen her daughter. Would she tell her mother about their meeting? Even that tenuous link with Lucy would give him vicarious pleasure. He had only told Eliza about his new career, his success, so that she would carry the news to Lucy. So that Lucy would think about him for at least a moment.

Alex pictured Lucy as she listened to Eliza, pictured her wide mouth saying rather casually, 'Oh. Alex. Really?' And the vividness of the image tortured him.

'Aagh,' he groaned and flung his head back against the seat. Clare, his companion, whom he had quite forgotten, turned to him.

'Dreadful junk, isn't it?' she whispered.

'What?' Alex tried to bring his attention back to the present. 'Yes, yes. Let's go. Come on. Let's go.' Impatiently, as if to drive away the image of Lucy's face, he stood up.

'Sshh.'

'Give over.'

'Look here.'

Clare took his elbow as he pushed his way out of the row.

Several rows behind them, Eliza started as Alex's head was superimposed for a second on the screen. It rested on the navel of the heroine's lovely body.

'Isn't that your friend?' Clare giggled and prodded Eliza.

'I'm not surprised he's leaving,' Eliza whispered stoutly. 'I think it's the most frightful rot.'

'We've paid all that money.'

'Oh, I don't want to leave.'

'Sshh.'

The two girls became silent and once more lifted their innocent eyes to the sordid scene. They looked like religious devotees thirsting for the Word.

But on the way home, Eliza thought again about her meeting with Alex. Her first instinct was to rush up to Lucy and tell her all about him, about his super new job, his super prosperous appearance, his super new girl friend . . . there was, however, *Lust for Blood*, to consider. Lucy had a talent for finding out every detail in a story and Eliza really didn't want her to know about that nasty film. This, at any rate, was the reason Eliza gave herself for not telling her mother about Alex; and if she hugged the memory of their meeting jealously to herself, it was only a minor self-deception.

Her father was, of course, another matter. He never asked awkward questions.

'You saw Alex? Darling.' Tom, sitting quietly in his study where Eliza had come to say good night, pushed aside the briefs he was studying. 'Not over here for long, I suppose?'

'Oh, no. He goes back tomorrow.'

'So his job's going well, then.'

'You know about it.' Eliza was disappointed that she couldn't surprise her father, but used to taking for granted his allknowingness. 'He says he's making pots of lovely money.'

'Good.' Tom reflected Eliza's smile of satisfaction. 'Then he won't be back for some time.'

'No. I suppose he won't.' Eliza who hadn't thought of it quite this way looked sadly at her feet which as usual seemed indelicately long, 'Well. Good night.'

Tom presented his cheek for her daughterly kiss. He was

genuinely glad for Alex's sake that he was doing well in his new career. He could never hate one of Lucy's lovers when they became so much part of the family. But he had acted as Alex's benefactor once more in order to keep him out of the country. Yes. He was glad he was doing well.

'Never mind, Lizzie. You'll be having real beaux soon.'

*

Lucy's new lover had come about quite naturally. As summer approached she had begun to feel restless. The liner which had used up so much of her energy for nearly a year was successfully completed, even triumphantly completed, and it only remained to be launched in a suitable jamboree of publicity. Lucy looked forward to this and yet was unsettled by the prospect. She started to turn away from Darrell who had given her all the help he could and to become aware of his sharp manner which had at first put her off. She felt the need of someone who mixed more easily with people, who would be a support to her at those publicity luncheons and cocktail parties. She certainly couldn't expect Tom to attend them.

Then she met Leo.

'Oh, I just sit around with my feet up most of the day.' When she first visited his office, Leo had sat in his leather swivel seat chair looking at his neatly shod feet placed high on his large slat-topped desk. He was in his mid-twenties but seemed younger, with bubbly yellow curls running down his neck. His physical beauty was what had first attracted Lucy to him and it was only an added bonus to discover that he was a creative director in a high-powered advertising agency. She was delighted to discover someone young and handsome who was also making money, and, it appeared, actually encouraged by her employers to spend theirs.

'Occasionally, I tip a bottle of Pouilly Fumé and twitch a speck of smoked salmon.' Lucy loved this languorous pose which was in such contrast to Darrell's intensity and she returned to his public school background (even if it was only a minor example) with a sigh of relief.

'But just now I feel like taking you to lunch at the Ritz.'

As for Leo, aside from Lucy's beauty which was always undeniable, he particularly enjoyed the sensation caused when he brought back to the agency this famous lady of the social columns.

'But how can you think in terms of thirty seconds? It's a flash. A spark. A quiver.' Lucy was always intrigued and excited by anything new and her restlessness abated.

Besides Leo was more democratic in bed than any of her previous lovers, which she found stimulating. For, although too much of a romantic to do anything as vulgar as comparing her beaux's performances, Lucy couldn't help noticing their different approaches. Tom was loving, Darrell was masterful and Leo expected every man to do his duty. She found it all rather jolly.

He took her to his flat which was large and pale and filled with cushions. Quite casually he would take off his clothes as if her presence there had very little to do with it. Such was his youthful charm that Lucy would lie back staring, quite forgetting to take off her own clothes or extract from him that loving homage that was generally so necessary to her. In fact she could not be so unselfconsciously naked as him, for at thirty-seven after three children, her body, though beautiful dancing under birch saplings in Scotland or swooning gracefully in a perfumed bath or turning in ecstasy on a bed of passion, had not the sculptural perfection for cold-blooded display. She waited therefore till Leo came to her and then mixed their golden curls upon the floor. How smooth was his body under her finger tips, how cleanly moulded, how young! Lucy felt herself dissolving on an ecstasy of perfection, as if Michelangelo's David had come alive to take her. And yet at the same time, she liked his matter-of-factness before and after their act of love. He did not bother to hide remnants of what she chose to believe were his past loves; the Indian cotton robe on the back of the bathroom door, the pile of hairclips in the cupboard, the old notes, 'Darling Leo, I've bought some butter.' She enjoyed it all and its air of freedom. Whether she would have been so happy if it had not been combined with a daytime reverence for her status and beauty is another matter.

*

Meanwhile, Eliza had taken her O Levels and gone to Paris. She stayed with a French family and attended classes at the Lycée. The whole experience was so strange to her that her separation from her mother caused no special heart-burning. As she became more capable of expressing herself in French, she found she was expressing in the different language, a different personality. She discovered she had views, likes and dislikes. She liked, for example, the son of the house who came home for the Christmas holiday which they spent in their country home in the Dordogne. Jules was twenty-one and very serious. They took walks together during which he lectured her on the French romantic poets with particular reference to Verlaine and she replied with recitations of Keats' 'Ode on a Grecian Urn'. When they came back to Paris where he was at college, he took her out for an occasional glass of wine and once even kissed her well-shaped mouth. Their relationship did not develop further because Jules was extremely correct and considered Eliza a child of the family and therefore an honorary sister. Instead he resorted to gallantry, bowing gracefully and referring to her as 'La Belle Anglaise'. Himself he called 'Le vieux gardien de la beauté'. All this flattered Eliza and she developed a charming air of self-confidence. At sixteen she seemed no longer a child but a young woman. It was with regret she saw summer coming to the Bois de Boulogne and realized her stay abroad was nearly over.

This second year which seemed so long to Eliza and was so important in her life was just more time passing quickly for her mother. True, within its compass she changed her lover and saw her biggest venture yet into commercial decorating be acclaimed a magnificent success. But basically she saw time as the enemy so that in order to avoid its grasp, she ignored its progress. She often protested that she chose her friends irrespective of age – which was true if her friends were taken to exclude her lovers, who though certainly not her own age were uniformly younger.

Lucy looked forward to Eliza's home-coming with the same love that she had always felt for her and a desire to fit her back once more into her home. In fact, although it was not her practice to admit even to herself regrets over the *status quo*, she had missed her admiring companionship more than she had expected.

Tom, unlike his wife, often thought about passing time and planned carefully for the future. Long ago, he had been impressed by the headmaster of his Catholic public school saying that he was educating the boys towards death. It was the contradiction in his character that he valued so highly Lucy's ability to live in the present. Warily he saw himself enjoying those two relatively tranquil years. Perhaps the startling youth and beauty of Leo added lines of age to his face and yet he had considered himself old for some time now. Besides, Leo with his charming if casual politeness and his easy manners with the servants and the younger children fitted more easily into the household – where Lucy soon brought him – than Darrell whose brusqueness had never endeared him to Tom's old-fashioned courtesy. Tom thought of himself as old and yet knew how much Lucy depended on him. More than that, how much she loved him. Without his presence she could not have carried on her life. So he was content.

Nevertheless he, even more than Lucy, looked forward to Eliza's return. After all, it had been his idea that she should go.

*

By an odd stroke of fate, Eliza's return to England was to coincide with Alex's.

Eliza thought she was unhappy after lengthy French farewells whose formality suited Jules' stern good looks. But once she was through the *Douane*, her mind turned forward to the excitement of seeing England and her own family again so that she did not notice a tall dark figure hurrying behind her. She recognized him as the boarding passengers crossed the tarmac to their plane. She only hesitated for a moment.

'Alex!' He turned round. Swinging her shoulder bag, leather tassels flying from her short jerkin, long legs dancing, Eliza caught up with him. 'Are you going to England too?'

Alex looked at her and saw the sort of lively attractive girl he spent money on in the evenings. It was delightful to feel her firm cheek pressed unselfconsciously against his.

'Where else on a day like this?'

Eliza laughed. 'It is a lovely day, isn't it? I've been in Paris for a year.'

Alex eyed her appreciatively, 'I can see that. You look terrific.'

'Do I? I'm so – so thrilled. It's quite odd to be speaking English. I haven't been back for a year.'

'I've been in Paris precisely eight hours.'

'Have you really?' Eliza found that almost as impressive as her year.

'My plane was diverted from Heathrow because of fog!'

'It seems a long diversion. Where were you coming from? America?'

'Yup. New York. Coming home, as a matter of fact.'

'Coming home?' Eliza looked at him eagerly. 'You mean, for good?'

'I don't know about that,' Alex smiled. 'For a few years anyway. I'm to be the English end of Wall Street.'

'Ah.' There were all kinds of questions Eliza wanted to ask, but at that moment they reached the plane and Alex was going first class. Eliza tossed her head, 'Mummy doesn't believe in spoiling her children.'

Alex stiffened. This charming new Eliza had obscured the fact that she was Lucy's daughter. Carefully and unnecessarily he transferred his briefcase from one hand to the other. By then he could look at Eliza again.

'Keep a seat for me and I'll come slumming.'

It was such an odd coincidence that Lucy's daughter should be the one to welcome him back to England, that Alex was struck afresh by the conviction that his life and Lucy's were still interlocked.

About six months ago he had discovered that it was Tom who had recommended him for his job. Far from making him angry, it had given him great satisfaction. For it had seemed to make him once more a member of the Trevelyan household, brought him once more into Lucy's orbit.

Lately, since he had known he would be returning to England, he had started writing to his sister for news of Lucy. Chloe realized she should not encourage her brother's continued obsessive interest but, with her own fatalistic approach to love, could not refuse. So she told him about Lucy's successes, about her changing beaux, her never-diminishing beauty.

Alex had never been able to regret the affair with Jessica because it had put him on equal terms with Lucy. He only regretted its consequences. His self-confidence, which had been shattered by their separation, mended itself under the flattering hands of other women – he never had difficulty in finding other willing women and now he was beginning to look for ways to end his banishment.

As he lurched down the plane towards Lucy's daughter, he couldn't help thinking he was going in the right direction. The First Class passengers' air hostess followed him with a bottle of champagne and two glasses.

Eliza sipped the champagne and felt a beatific glow spread across her face. It was like a dream to be flying home to her mother and her family with Alex as her escort. Her childhood hero-worship for him had only changed enough for her to see in an adult way how charming and handsome he was; how witty and amusing.

'And how is your mother?' asked Alex after a couple of glasses.

'I haven't seen her for a year.'

'Cast into outer darkness.'

'Not at all. She writes wonderful letters. I used to translate them into French and make everyone fall about laughing. All about telly commercials, glue used for hairspray, shadows used for stains, you know the sort of thing.'

'I didn't know your mother was involved in that sort of thing?' Alex lied encouragingly.

'Oh, she isn't. She's got this friend who is. Leo . . .'

'I see. Leo.' Alex became silent. Although Chloe had written about Leo, it was a shock to hear his name spoken so gaily.

'Leo the Lion. You're Taurus, aren't you?'

'The bull. And your mother's Virgo.'

'Yes. Anyway, you can see her when we arrive. They'll all be meeting me.'

'No,' said Alex, suddenly. Eliza stared. 'I mean. Let's keep it between us, our meeting like this.'

Eliza was suddenly reminded of their meeting in Leicester Square. Then, she had kept it secret from her mother. For some reason she felt her cheeks turn pink at the thought.

'It's a funny coincidence us being on the same plane, isn't it? I mean if your plane hadn't been diverted . . .'

'Yes.' Alex looked across at her soft rosy face and thought as he had at first how pretty she was and yet now it only seemed the shadow of Lucy's beauty. 'It must be Kismet,' he said lightly and then, some instinct making him sure it was important, he repeated again, 'Let's keep it between us.'

'But they'll see you.'

'I'm very good at hiding.'

'I'll feel like a spy.'

'A very beautiful spy.' Alex gently took her hand.

A faraway look came into Eliza's eyes. It was the first time anyone had called her beautiful in English.

Alex's insistence on hiding from Lucy made his first sight of her more agonizing. He made the ridiculous comparison between himself and Lucifer, both of them, as he had said about Eliza earlier, being 'cast into outer darkness', away from Lucy's shining presence. And yet he only partly saw the absurdity of the comparison.

Lucy, golden curls lifted in tendrils round her bright eyes and glowing cheeks, ran to meet her daughter. She was even more extraordinary, more full of life than Alex had remembered. For a moment Chloe's sharp face came before him and he thought of her impassioned lack of understanding when she had learnt of the Jessica affair, 'Why did you spoil the golden goose, Alex? Why did you do it? She gave you everything. Her home, her family, her body, even her love, as much as she was able. Why couldn't you be content?'

Now Ticky and Rupert were dancing round their sister, shouting in their excitement, trying to drag along her cases.

'No! Rupert. Ticky. Darling. You'll hurt yourself.'

Only Tom was missing. He was probably working, as it was near the end of the summer term and the courts would be busy. It was easy for Alex to picture him there, at his desk or in court, his brain fully employed by his work but somewhere at the back of his mind, a continuous awareness of Lucy, of his family. Alex had never really tried to understand Tom. For one thing, too much understanding might have worried his conscience; for another, the thirty-year age-gap made him seem a remote figure, more like a father than a rival. He vaguely assumed Lucy had made an agreement with her husband and left it at that. Husbands didn't drive Lucy around in the daytime. Alex knew that well. Lovers did.

Warily, he followed Lucy out of the airport and immediately saw Leo. He sat at the wheel of Lucy's Rover. Furiously, he noticed how his yellow hair matched Lucy's yellow car. She waved at him gaily.

'Leo's very kindly driving us,' Alex heard her explaining to Eliza. Unable to bear the sight any longer, he turned away. He therefore missed the anxious eager look Eliza gave the airport, before she got into the car.

PART II

'These violent delights have violent ends,
And in their triumph die, like fire and powder,
Which, as they kiss, consume.'

Romeo and Juliet, Act II, scene vi

6

Eliza was preparing to go to a dance. She pushed bangles up her slim arms and combed her mass of black hair into a cloak around her pointed shoulders. She swayed her naked hips in the mirror and the silver button she'd glued to her navel glittered exotically. It was a fancy-dress dance and she was going as a harem girl.

'How do I look? How do I look?' On light-thonged sandals she ran up to her mother's room.

'I'm in here, darling.' Lucy lay in her bath, soaking away her working worrying self. 'Oh, how glorious! How dazzling!'

'I am. I am.' Eliza felt joyous. 'And you are too,' she added generously. 'You look so soft and squeezy in the bath.'

Lucy made a slight grimace and then rallied, 'Darling, why don't you borrow my Indian earrings with all the dangly bits.'

'Do you think so?' Eliza was considering. She went through to Lucy's dressing-table. 'No, they're not right on me,' she called after a pause. 'They look tarty; my face is too small or something.'

Downstairs in the drawing-room, Eliza's escort, a young man of impeccable manners and antecedents, fingered his daring bow tie (it was navy blue) nervously.

'Oh, heavens! Jamie! Have I kept you waiting ages!' Eliza flew in on wings of confidence. She had left her chrysalis far behind.

'It was worth it,' Jamie bowed, gallantly hiding his shock at her semi-nudity.

'But you're not in fancy dress. Oh, why aren't you dressed up?' Eliza felt the evening's perfection suddenly threatened.

'Men look silly dolled up.'

'Oh.'

'Only poofs wear drag.' This argument was clearly incontestable.

'Yes. Of course.' Eliza was relieved to be happy again. She saw it was very cool of Jamie to wear evening clothes. 'Shall we be off, then?'

'Rightio.' Jamie followed her into the hall and carefully wound her slim body into a large cloak. He had decided with a seventeen-year-old's sense of priorities that her daring costume would impress his friends, 'God. You'll make Eddie and Adrian mad with desire.'

'Good.' Eliza pulled free her hair with a satisfied smile. She wanted public acclaim. 'We're off, Mummy!' she called up the stairs.

'Have fun, darling. But remember what happened to Cinderella at midnight.'

'Oh, Mummy,' Eliza made a face at Jamie. 'It doesn't finish till two.'

'See you tomorrow, then.'

'Bye!'

'Good-bye, Mrs Trevelyan.' They slammed the door behind them.

Upstairs, Lucy, following a sentimental mother's instinct, drew back the curtains in her bedroom and watched as her daughter set off for her first big night out. The M.G.B., going much too fast, roared away down the road and she withdrew from the winter night. Returning to the dressing-table, she sat down slowly. There in front of her lay the dangly earrings Eliza had rejected. She had offered them to Eliza because they had always brought her luck and compliments to herself. Eliza had called them 'tarty'. She held them up to her face and they looked as pretty as ever.

*

By midnight the ballroom had resolved itself into a whirligig of colour and movement. Original patterns of dinner parties and partners had disappeared into a more fluid shape and poor Jamie had lost hope of ever reclaiming his harem girl.

Eliza was dancing with a tall, dark man.

Alex said, 'Aren't you rather young for this sort of thing?'

'I'm nearly seventeen.'

'It seems impossible.'

'I expect you mean because of Mummy. Really it's very awkward.' Eliza had been drinking wine for four hours and was seeing life very clearly.

Alex laughed. 'Who brought you here?'

'Oh, a boy.' She waved her hand negligently. 'He's hovering around somewhere.'

Alex was genuinely charmed by this young virgin whom he described satirically to himself as 'bounding on the threshold of womanhood'. Yet he could not separate her from thoughts of her mother. Everything she said or did echoed Lucy in a way which was a mixture of pain and pleasure.

'How do you manage to be so black and beautiful, when your mother's so fair and beautiful?'

'We're night and day. Rose red and snow white. And anyway Mummy's not really as blonde as all that.'

'What a terrible insinuation.' Alex smiled but his continuing sense of the homage due to Lucy was really shocked that such a little mouse should dare to nibble at the pedestal. For a moment it brought Eliza into sharper focus.

'Is London living up to your expectations?'

'Well, we only just got back from summer holidays in Scotland. I'm not sure. I haven't done much before tonight.'

'Perhaps I can help,' said Alex, partly meaning it and partly mechanically, for at the mention of Scotland his imagination had swept him out to pictures of Lucy on Scottish moors. He remembered climbing up a steep slope with her and finding at the top a little shepherd's hut. They had gone in to its sheep-smelling darkness and, lying down on the earth floor, made such romantic love.

He looked down into Eliza's large blue eyes.

'You haven't been listening,' she accused him.

'The music's so loud. Let's sit down. And I'll plan some entertainment for you.'

'Daddy's never taken me to the Old Bailey. I'd love to go there.'

'No. No, that's his treat. I'm not in that scene any more. I'll think of something else.'

'Oh, do. Please. Something different.'

Alex looked at her flushed and excited face. She was so pretty. How could he resist? Lucy's daughter handing herself to him with open eager eyes. Still he had no fixed intentions, only the need to get closer to Lucy.

He leant towards Eliza and caught the smell of her young, heated body.

'How about Madame Tussaud's for a start?'

'Oh, no! As a child, I was taken there whenever it rained.'

'As a child?' Alex laughed, and seeing in her more of Lucy than ever before felt a correspondingly greater interest.

*

Lucy prided herself on her understanding of the human psyche; with the unmentionable exception of Alex, no one had ever stepped out of the role in which she had cast them. She knew there were parts of her own character which she found it easier to veil from herself, but she never did the same with other people. Thus she never expected there would be any reason to interfere in Eliza's adult life. At an early age she had given her the biological details of sex but had not added any direct moral guidelines. Lucy could not say 'this is right' and 'this is wrong', because she did not believe life was like that. Eliza's years of careful upbringing should have taught her how to behave and it was too late if they hadn't. She gave her complete independence, in the confidence there would be no unpleasant surprises. Personally she was quite prepared for Eliza's growing into a woman. In fact she looked forward to the 'best friend' her daughter would surely become to her.

Therefore after her initial surprise at her transformation after a year abroad, she had reacted only with encouragement and admiration. Certain as Lucy was of her own supreme beauty and intelligence she could never have been jealous. She was delighted to see Eliza pretty, happy, bouncing with life and energy, just as she was delighted to see the little Ticky set up a doll's tea party. She looked forward to meeting Eliza's boyfriends and greeted such as Jamie of the blue bow tie with gracious charm. However, there was one thing she had not expected; that Eliza should find herself a steady boyfriend but keep him secret from her family. She had suspected almost at once that Eliza had found someone special and waited eagerly to see who it was. When after a couple of weeks no information was forthcoming, she began to get restless. Eventually she spoke to Tom, although only in the lightest of tones.

'Have you realized Lizzie's in love, darling?'

They were sitting in the drawing-room on a dank Sunday. Lucy was listening to *The Magic Flute* to elevate her thoughts, but the magic did not seem to be getting through.

'It's much more fun for her, of course. But I do wish she'd bring him home. It's so unlike her to be secretive.'

Tom looked up from a pile of papers. 'She's probably shy. Once she's got two or three she won't care so much. The first one's always hardest.'

'How clever of you. I suppose it's true. Can you remember the first girl you fell in love with?' Lucy, feeling more relaxed, slipped off her shoes and wiggled her toes childishly.

'Perfectly. She was tall with golden curls and pink cheeks and every other man in London was in love with her too.'

'That's not fair. I was going to reminisce about Julian who made his first Holy Communion on the same day I did. And how we held hands up the aisle and I was all dressed in white with a veil so that I felt just like a bride. It took me days to get over him.'

'You're more generous than I.' Tom leant over and squeezed her hand. 'And more beautiful.' He returned to his papers.

But for once Lucy was not satisfied with such an ending to the conversation. Although she really and truly liked the idea of the lovely Eliza finding a boyfriend, she did want him to become part of the household. As her lovers did.

'I do hate anything that seems underhand.'

'What?'

'Nothing.' Lucy stood up defeatedly. 'Shall we have a drink, darling?'

But now Tom looked at her more attentively.

'Why don't you ask her, if you're worried it's someone unsuitable? She's so honest she'd always answer a direct question.'

Faced with the idea of cross-questioning her daughter,

Lucy realized how she was exaggerating the situation and suddenly felt calmer.

'Of course she would. I'm being absurd. The trouble is with no big job on, my imagination's not fully employed.' It was a relief to think of herself again. She wondered if this was the moment to tell Tom of Leo's plans for her – queen of the advertising world, it was an amusing idea – she smiled; but decided to leave Tom in peace a little longer.

'Whisky, darling?'

*

Eliza danced behind her mother who was sitting at her dressing-table. She was wearing a long skirt which flicked round her slim ankles. She'd tied her hair in two plaits which bounced over her shoulders.

'Mummy, I do like your hair like that, I really do.'

Keeping very still, Lucy touched the blonde coils which had been pinned exotically to the back of her head. She was just going off to do a television interview and cared even more about her appearance than usual.

'They wanted to put a comb in, but I decided against it.'

'Oh, no. It's perfect now. With that high neckline.'

Lucy smiled. 'Darling, you are sweet. I hope your boy-friend's as complimentary as you.'

Eliza blushed and then smoothed the end of one of her plaits across her cheek. Finally she smiled too. 'He's a great admirer of yours.'

'Of mine?'

'Oh, yes. You're quite a public figure. Lots of people I meet know about you.'

'I'd love to meet him.'

'He's frightened of you. You know.'

'Not at all.'

Lucy peered at the mirror for one last check. She parted her lips at her reflection.

'But you needn't worry. He's just your type.'

'*Un tipo?*' Lucy watched her white teeth appear between her pink lips. She must remember not to smile too widely during the interview. Women were not taken seriously unless they took themselves seriously.

'I think you've got the best taste in the world!' said Eliza suddenly.

'Oh, heavens.'

'But, I do. I couldn't do better than follow your example.' Eliza shut her mouth tight, as if she had said everything by that. But Lucy, mind on the approaching challenge, merely held out her cheek for a farewell kiss.

'And do get Rupert straight into bed after the programme, won't you, darling?'

'I bet you'll be wonderful,' Eliza generously returned from contemplating her own life to her mother's. 'You always are.'

'Thank you, darling. I do hope this hair stays. See you later.'

*

'I saw Eliza the other day,' said Chloe. 'She certainly has grown up into a beauty. Not that it's any surprise.' Chloe was having her early-morning telephone conversation with Lucy. She was feeling dismal herself because it looked as if her present married man would stay married and she had been allowing herself to consider the prospect of becoming a mother herself. The man in question had told her how much he would love her smooth round tummy. She belted her dressing-gown more tightly. 'Children grow up so quickly.'

Lucy was lying in bed. White frills cascaded round her bosom and elbows. 'It's like gardening. There's always more coming along behind.'

'You're not...?' began Chloe jealously.

'No. Thank God. I meant Ticky and Rupert.' She pushed the frills up her white arm, 'You know, Eliza has a boy-friend.'

'That must make you feel old.'

'Not at all.' Lucy laughed. 'I fear it's some ragged stu-dent, quite unsuitable. She says he's frightened of me and won't bring him home.'

'No daughter of yours could have bad taste.'

'That's what Eliza said. More or less. She seems to think I'm the arbiter of good taste in men. A sort of Good Men Guide.'

Chloe laughed. But Lucy became uneasy. Something in what Eliza had said started some lingering worry. But she could not at all think what it was. She wished she had not been taken up by that stupid television interview during the nearest Eliza had got to a heart-to-heart.

'As long as he's not married.' Chloe grimaced to herself.

'Oh, no. She didn't speak about him like that. I'd have known if it was that. Heavens, I'm sounding quite silly and menopausal.'

'You never could.' Chloe became more gloomy. She compared her own fruitless life with Lucy's ever-fruitful. In order to cheer herself up she reminded herself that she was at least a good photographer. 'Don't forget my exhibition. You're to be the grand climax. No. 100. In the full flush of your beauty. Do you remember, in the garden?'

'Yes. Yes.' Lucy seemed untypically vague about a photograph of herself.

'How's Alex?' she asked unexpectedly.

Chloe was too startled to react for a moment, 'I thought you couldn't bear to mention Bluebeard's name.'

'I can't. It's just that ... something made me think ...' Lucy's voice died away.

'He's all right.' Chloe was matter-of-fact. 'He was in

America. And now he's back. Looking very prosperous. I haven't seen him much. I expect he's got some bird in tow he thinks I won't approve of.'

'Yes.' Lucy's face, which had hardened into lines of tension, smoothed. She felt obscurely relieved at the idea that Alex was occupied with a girl. She glanced at the jewelled clock on her bedside table. 'I must get going, darling. I've one of those dynamic days meeting the Mayor of London.'

'There was something else. About Eliza. You wouldn't mind if I photographed her, would you? I'd just like to catch her, before she matures.'

'Matures? You sound like a dirty magazine. Of course you can. You always have.'

'Yes. Good.' Chloe wondered why she had asked Lucy's permission with such formality. It had obviously irritated her. Or perhaps she was still thinking of Alex. Now it was her turn to be touched by an uneasy premonition. Alex's intensity over Lucy had begun to frighten her, so that it was a relief when he no longer came to her with his echoing questions. She had been glad to decide he was getting over his madness, perhaps falling in love again. But why had Lucy mentioned him after such a long silence? Chloe shook her straight hair round her face. It was too early in the morning for dark thoughts. Instead, she pictured Lucy superbly *grande dame* at her mayoral banquet; pink and perfect and quite remote from all unpleasantness.

'Well, keep your necklaces simple,' she said brightly. 'You know how jealous mayors get.'

'I always wear pearls for mayors,' Lucy replied with equal gaiety. And they both put down their receivers.

*

Eliza's face was filled with exultation; her eyes were glazed and staring, her lips were moist and parted, her cheeks flushed. As she reached a crescendo of pleasure, she shut her eyes.

Alex glanced at her and even in the dim light could see the depth of her emotion. It made him feel very old. He sighed and looked away again. If he had loved her it might have been different.

The final chords of Brahms' Violin Concerto spun vibrating in the air and then died slowly away.

'Oh!' gasped Eliza in the pause before the audience broke into thunderous applause. Alex squeezed her hand. It was warm and damp like a child's.

They both blinked as the lights went up.

'That was marvellous!' breathed Eliza, quicker to return to herself than Alex had expected. 'And now let's walk along the embankment and watch the lights in the water and then cross the bridge with the water below us . . .'

Alex was filled with such sadness as they walked beside the dark river that he could hardly bear to listen to Eliza's enthusiasm.

'Music makes me feel I could do anything in the world. Be anything. Do anything. For example, if I stood on that parapet now I could do the most perfect swallow dive into the Thames so that a crowd would gather and throw bouquets at me. And then I'd swim and somersault and dance in the water like a nymph and then I'd catch a silver tassel hooked to a cloud, except there aren't any, and I'd pull myself up like a brilliant trapeze artist and I'd be dressed all in glittering sequins. And I'd swing right to the top of . . .' she waved her arm to look for a suitable object, 'to the top of the highest pinnacle of the House of Lords!'

Alex smiled, 'And what would I do while you were away among the stars?'

Eliza looked reflective. 'I'm not sure about you. I can't do other people yet. I'm only on stage one.' She brightened.

'Mummy can though, she can make anyone be anything she wants. It's she who really makes me into a . . .'

'Trapeze artist?'

'Why don't you take me seriously?' Eliza pouted and then laughed. 'I know I'm ridiculous but I'm so happy. And it's true about Mummy. She made me see how perfect you were. How clever. How handsome. How charming . . .' Eliza looked up at Alex earnestly.

He tried to lose his smile. 'And you wouldn't have thought those things otherwise?'

'That's not the point. It's too difficult to explain. I wish you'd let me bring you home. It seems so silly, all this secrecy. It's the sort of thing Mummy hates, too.'

Alex walked away from her and leant over the bridge. He liked the feel of the hard stone pressing against his chest. He had not precisely envisaged this dicing with his emotions, this playing with Eliza so that she fell in love with him while he only looked for her mother. Now he found the pain of it was beginning to outweigh the pleasure. He could hardly bear to touch her, although she was more and more eager. Instead of reminding him of Lucy she reminded him that she was not Lucy, however much she was like her. Instead of being pleased or even amused by her adoration he was merely irritated by her childlike lack of discrimination. Everything he said or did was perfect. And now he knew she wanted him to make love to her. Far from finding it a tempting prospect, he felt a kind of revulsion – as if at incest. To him it would be incest. Besides he didn't want to make the same mistake he had made over Jessica. He didn't want to punish Lucy, he wanted to have her.

Sometimes when he felt most pressured by Eliza's demanding looks, he was tempted to tell her about Jessica, about her mother. And yet she was his only hope, his only link with Lucy.

He turned back to Eliza. She wanted him to come to her mother's house. Well, what was he waiting for?

'I will come, Eliza. Home.'

'You will! You will! How wonderful.' Eliza's long hair whipped Alex's face as she danced around him in exultation. He moved aside slightly. 'That will be wonderful really. I just know Mummy will be overwhelmed.'

'With delight?'

'Oh, Alex. Of course. Come on, I'm starving. Let's get something to eat.'

*

'No. No. Move. Talk. Don't think about the camera at all.'

'But it's so difficult,' Eliza objected. 'How can I forget that great black thing's peering at me?'

Chloe was trying to capture the young passionate look that she had seen in Eliza but she wondered if it was too late. Already she wanted to fix her face into that same madonna-like shield of perfect beauty that Lucy always adopted. It was probably not a conscious imitation, but still hard to break down.

'Talk,' she said again.

'What about?' Eliza was wearing a long white robe and a velvet ribbon tied round her throat; with her dark hair rippling over her shoulders, she was like some Victorian heroine.

'Tell me about your boyfriend.'

At once Eliza's face flooded with pink and her enormous blue eyes glistened as if filling with tears. Her lips quivered and the immobility of a pale statue changed to the vibrating sensibility of a young girl. Delighted, Chloe clicked her camera; this was what she had hoped for.

'How do you know? I mean who told you?' Eliza's flush died slowly away, but her fingers played nervously with her hair.

'Your mother,' Chloe replied carelessly, intent on catching the delicate white fingers entwined in the dark hair.

'Mummy! You mean she knows?' Eliza gaped in astonishment.

'She's no fool. Lucy. Your mother.'

'No.' Gradually a look of satisfaction smoothed out Eliza's features. 'And she's pleased?'

'Well, she'd like to know who he is.'

'Who he is?' Eliza was bewildered. She had thought her mother knew; that it was all straight. That all Alex's horrid secrecy could be abandoned.

'Hang on. Must change the film.' Chloe, dashing enthusiastically across her studio, did not notice Eliza's sudden disappointment. For a moment she stood still and then, seeming to make up her mind, followed Chloe who was now crouched on the floor over her camera.

'But ... Listen. It's Alex!' Eliza shook her shoulder almost crossly. It had all become too much for her. Alex had never said she couldn't tell his sister. 'It's your brother who's taking me out!'

Chloe sat back on her heels. At once she saw the inevitability of it. She was amazed at herself for not guessing before. It was so incredibly obvious. Desperately she tried to think what it meant. How serious was it? How serious was Eliza? How serious was Alex?

'I see,' she said weakly.

'You see. You see,' Eliza cried excitedly. 'You're his sister. You know how wonderful he is. We have such good times together. But he won't let me tell Mummy. Although I think he will soon. At least he said he'd come to the house which is a start at any rate.'

'Yes.' Mechanically, Chloe finished loading her camera and stood up. She tried to smile at Eliza. 'Yes. Your mother will soon find out, if he comes to the house.'

'Of course, we're not very big here. I said over the phone . . .'

'It's the garden we want to see.'

'The garden. But we haven't got a . . .' Mr Douche recovered himself nobly, 'It's not the best time of year.'

'We all have the same problem,' said Lucy sympathetically.

'They didn't say the yard . . .' Once more Mr Douche stopped in confusion and welcomed with relief his wife who came in with a tea tray.

'I thought you might be cold after a drive like that.'

'They want to see the garden, Ann.'

'The yard . . .'

'The garden, dear.'

'I'd better take the dustbins out, then. They didn't collect this week.'

Lucy tried to make her smile seem mere politeness,

'Don't worry Mrs Doochay, please. It's just the size and shape we're interested in. Don't move a thing.'

'If I'd have known. That is, if you could come back in the spring when I have a few narcissi and later there's our new yellow rose – put in to cover where the pipes stained the wall – it's called King's Ransom.' She looked at them hopefully. It was obvious to her that if she let them set foot in her garden the game was up.

'Through the kitchen, I'm afraid,' apologized Mr Douche.

'Interesting. Very interesting.' Leo looked round the grey concrete yard appreciatively.

'It is a nice regular shape,' Mr Douche was still doing his best. His wife eyed Leo, who was carefully measuring the tiny space, as if he'd dropped from another planet.

'It's certainly down the market,' he said and Mr Douche

looked pleased at the compliment. 'A shot or two through the windows.'

'They're lovely windows,' agreed Lucy, 'perfect. Take in the kettle steaming on the stove.'

'Slice of life ... backlighting. Get the right director,' mused Leo. 'Thank you very much then,' he swung round decisively, 'for showing us.'

'And for the tea,' said Lucy, shaking hands, 'I haven't had such a good cuppa for ages.'

'Yes,' Mrs Douche stared at Lucy's radiant face in its nest of fur and thought she was already part of a film. 'Are you ... I mean, you must be the star,' she said wonderingly.

'My wife makes a very good cup of tea,' Mr Douche brought back the subject in hand. 'Real old-fashioned strong-brewed; none of that dreadful washing-up water tea-bag stuff!'

'It's a tea-bag commercial, dear,' said Leo heartlessly, and Lucy had to hide behind a handkerchief.

*

'This film could be so real,' said Leo as the car roared away from the little house.

'If only it doesn't snow,' Lucy looked up at the darkening sky and sank further into her coat.

'No problem. Just sweep it off ... bang in a few lights. Get the right cameraman.'

'Mad. Mad.'

Lucy had joined a section of society that went to greater lengths to create a world of everlasting beauty than she did herself. Perhaps she had found the job most suited to her talents.

'You were like a child in there. Giggling.'

'Oh dear. Did I spoil your sense of importance?'

'How do you manage to be everything, Lucy? You'll spoil other women for me.'

'I should hope so.'

'A woman, a girl, a child, a friend, a colleague . . .'

'Custom does not stale her infinite variety,' Lucy laughed. But Leo was serious.

'What's your secret? An intellectual like you . . . Give me the breakdown.'

'Plenty of love and a clear conscience. But that's only because I'm Catholic.'

'God as well. It's hardly playing the game.'

'And how about you? You're free, young, clever, successful, beautiful . . .'

'Oh, Lucy. Lucy.'

The car took them inexorably back to London and the cold evening air froze their features.

'I can't feel you,' said Lucy when they stopped a street away from her house and he tried to kiss her.

'That's the trouble,' said Leo.

'Nonsense!' Lucy jumped gaily out of the car. 'We'll speak tomorrow.'

'I'm not sure I like this business relationship,' shouted Leo after her, 'it seems to keep us to office hours.'

'Very salutary for us both,' called Lucy waving her fur-gloved hand. And indeed she was in the best of spirits. She ran and watched her breath pant out into white swirls in the dusk. The days were short now and she was quite surprised to see her pale house loom out of the dusky sky.

'Oh.' She stopped suddenly outside her front garden. A man's figure had just crossed the paving and descended to the basement. It could only be Eliza's mysterious boyfriend. The urge to summon him back out of the gloom was overwhelming but her principles held. She despised above all the prying mother. Eliza must bring him to her when she was ready. And yet his shadowy figure was a shadow on her day.

*

In fact Alex had heard her approaching steps which he would have recognized whatever the circumstances and he had felt sure it was the moment of confrontation. His heart had bounded in a ludicrous schoolboy way and then, when there had been no summons, sunk like lead. Once inside the house, he had become so depressed that even Eliza had noticed it. It was the first time he had come in with her, and she drew what seemed to her the obvious conclusion.

'I suppose it seems awfully *infra dig* to be sitting down here in my little room after being all exotically above stairs.'

She was too near the truth for Alex to make any very sensible rejoinder.

'I like being with you,' he said.

'Honestly?'

'You cheer me up.'

'I never think of you as gloomy.'

'That's because you only see me when I'm with you.'

'Except just now. You looked quite miserable.'

'That's because I'd only arrived a moment ago, so your influence hadn't started working.'

'You win. I'll change the subject. How about giving me a lecture on *Macbeth*? I've got an essay on The Symbolism of Night.'

'I'm too lazy.' Alex took off his shoes and stretched out along her bed. He really did look exhausted.

'Have you been working too hard?' Eliza seemed genuinely concerned though generally she spurned illness or tiredness. Lucy had taught her that such weaknesses were best carried away from the public eye. Only her wish for intimacy with Alex made her sympathize.

Alex was thinking that the last time he lay on the bed, it had been to seduce Eliza's friend, Jessica. Normally he avoided situations that might give Eliza's big blue eyes a chance to languish desirously. But today he felt too tired. Tired and yet reckless.

Eliza knelt down beside him,

'Shall I stroke your forehead?'

Alex closed his eyes and felt her childish hand smooth back his hair.

'I used to do it for Daddy a lot. But I don't so much now.' She giggled slightly. 'It's much more fun doing it to you.'

'I bet it is.' But Alex had lost his usual defensive tone of badinage and the words sounded like encouragement.

'I can massage too,' Eliza continued softly, leaning further over his chest and slipping her hand round his neck.

Alex shuddered. What an irony if he should now be seduced by Lucy's daughter. Who would believe that? And yet her sixteen-year-old's breasts were pressing close to him and her breath was on his face. At least it wouldn't be illegal. He tried to smile but it turned into a sigh. If only it had been Lucy. 'Go on, Eliza, angel.' He put up an arm and gently pushed her back. 'I'm too exhausted, honestly.'

Eliza pouted but was not offended. Her overtures were only partly serious for she sensed that something made Alex safe and she played with him like a tame bear. She would have been truly terrified if he had rolled his bulk on top of her.

Alex, understanding something of this, admonished

himself for his fantasy. He must not give Eliza her mother's characteristics. It was dangerous, dangerous.

'Give me a kiss, then.' Eliza pursed her pink mouth prettily.

She played games, like a child with no understanding of anything. Abruptly Alex sat himself upright.

'Come here. Just a quick one. I must be off.'

'Off? But you've only just arrived!' Eliza forgot the kiss in her surprise.

Alex stamped his feet into his shoes.

'Well, you can come too. I'm only going to a film.'

'Great. Which one? Hold on. I must brush my hair.'

Alex had suddenly felt a claustrophobic terror of being trapped in Eliza's bedroom. He wanted Lucy to find out about them but not this evening in the warm intimacy of her own basement. He would choose his own time and place.

*

The following afternoon at about five o'clock, Lucy was coming out of her dressmaker's. It was already dark and as she walked slowly towards her house a few streets away, she was thinking only the most trivial romantic thoughts. Christmas in Scotland was approaching and she liked to picture how it would be. How the long silk kaftan she had just been trying on would shine against the purple cushions in her drawing-room; how she would order muffins and heather honey for tea, after Tom and whoever else they invited had come in from shooting; how she would organize an expedition to ski in the mountains if the snow fell; how Leo would keep her company in icy walks; in short, how lovely her well-earned Christmas would be.

So it took her some time to become aware of a tall figure dogging her footsteps. In the end Alex came right up to her. Just before he did and lost all sense in gazing at her face, he wondered for a sharp flash what Tom's attitude to his reappearance would be. But who could think of Lucy's husband when Lucy herself was there?

She glanced sideways at him and he saw the blank surprise in her eyes. He waited for her look of recognition.

'I'm going your way,' he said, as calmly as he could.

But Lucy remained blank-faced for she was trying to decide whether she would even speak to him. Yet silence could be even more telling. She must at once reduce their meeting from the dangerous emotional level she sensed from his drawn face. She must show he meant nothing more to her than a casual acquaintance almost forgotten. She would be polite, conversational.

'It's almost too cold for walking.' She found herself shivering and pulled her fur coat close round her neck.

'Yes.' Alex had nothing to say, for their steps, as they moved in time towards her house, would soon carry them to all the explanation necessary.

'What a coincidence,' said Lucy as he continued beside her, 'that your way should be the same as mine.' And she thought how convincingly cheerful she sounded, when beside her walked the man who had tried to destroy her life. Yet he seemed so pale and tongue-tied. She wondered if she could ever feel sorry for him. She turned to him to say good-bye for they had reached the entrance to her house and in that moment she understood. His large dark eyes looked beyond her. Then, bending, he opened the ornamental gate. He stood aside to let her through.

'Ah,' Lucy gasped. She felt as if all the vibrancy of life had drained away into the hard stone paving. She looked down, suddenly thinking in a mad way to see it sprout with some strange flower, or perhaps hoping that when she looked up again Alex would be gone.

But he stood rooted to the ground. His eyes fixed on her face and in the weird light of the street lamp they seemed like a madman's. He seized her arm.

'I had to.'

'What?' Lucy whispered. She had not yet the strength to be angry but her voice shook with a sort of derision. 'You had to? With my daughter?'

Her voice hissed out at Alex and if he had not been past all common caring, he would have quailed under such scorn. Instead he persisted in the course he had chosen.

'She loves me.'

'My daughter,' repeated Lucy and she felt about Eliza as she had when she was a baby. 'She's part of me.' Her voice rose suddenly and she shook her arm free of his. 'How could you? How could you? How could you?'

Alex moved slightly as if to break the spell of this wild chant and a new thought struck Lucy. It struck her quite still so that Alex approached her again and put out his hand.

'I love you, Lucy.'

But Lucy was so bound up with the new horror that she did not hear his words.

'Have you, have you ...?' But after all she could not put it into words.

Alex didn't answer for a moment but it was only because he hadn't understood her meaning. Then he whirled round as if he might after all run from her,

'You didn't used to be so prissy,' he shouted. 'Do you mean, have I fucked your daughter? Eliza's very pretty, you know. Quite takes after her mother in lots of ways. Just dying for it. Tongue hanging out. All fresh and juicy ...'

'Shut up!' shouted Lucy. 'Shut up! Shut up!'

This was not how Alex had pictured their meeting. This loud brawling. This awful vulgarity. All he had wanted was to take her in his arms, to be allowed to love her. But she was shouting at him as if he was a child. His heart which had been burning with love, warming his whole body, seemed to freeze. If this was how she wanted it, she would find him as icily determined as herself.

'It's no good,' he said quietly. 'I'm here. And you can't make me disappear.'

And then they both saw Eliza.

Eliza looked from one to the other, now silent, apart. She burst out,

'Oh, I'm so glad! You've met at last. Isn't he a marvellous wonderful surprise?' She had only just come up from the basement and had heard nothing more than loud words. She seemed to think they had been cries of surprised delight. She skipped towards Lucy whose face had fixed in an expression of bewilderment. 'Do you see why I said he was your type? I was sure you'd guess then, but Alex was so keen to hide himself away that I didn't dare do more than hint. It's so funny, isn't it, that I should bring him back into the family after so long.' She looked slowly across to the still figure of Alex.

'Two years,' said Lucy, putting her hand on Eliza's shoulder. 'We'll all freeze if we stay out here much longer. I need a cup of tea,' she looked at Alex ironically, 'or perhaps a glass of champagne.'

'To celebrate.' Alex returned her look and took a step forward. Hastily Lucy retreated to the front door but her way was blocked by Eliza.

'I'm so happy everything's straight now!' she cried, almost hugging her mother.

Alex strode towards the two women and put an arm round each. Even though he could feel Lucy's shoulder stiffen it was an unbelievable joy to touch her once again. He thought to himself that no one could resist love like his.

*

They had arranged to meet in the same restaurant that had been the prelude to so many afternoons of love. It was a small undistinguished trattoria, which had become fashionable only after Lucy's patronage. Because of her patronage. Lucy did not want to be reminded, but Alex had insisted and she was in no position to refuse. He arrived a quarter of an hour early in order to enjoy the anticipation of her arrival. When it came her beauty almost took his breath away. If she'd implored immediately, if you love me, leave me and my family alone, he might have agreed.

But Lucy was defiant. The beauty he admired was deliberate; she had chosen her most dazzling dress and been to the hairdresser. She wanted to overawe him into disappearing.

'What will you drink?' asked Alex politely. For himself he needed no more than her presence.

'Champagne.' Lucy slipped off her fur cloak that she had brought to her seat. She ignored the waiter who held out his hand to take the cloak from her. Already she had been irritated by the patron's enthusiastic welcome and his presumptuous, 'It is a long time since we see the Signorina here.' She had used to enjoy being 'the Signorina'. Now she looked round the restaurant as if expecting to recognize friends and, when there was no one, sighed disparagingly, 'This restaurant's gone downhill.' As Alex made no answer except to stare at her she opened the menu too lovingly pressed on her by yet another waiter and decided, carelessly, 'I shall have cold lobster.' It was much the most expensive dish on the menu. But despite this defiance her heart was sinking at the impassive adoring face across the table. It seemed beyond words or reason.

Lucy took a sip of the champagne and then anxiety overcame prudence. She had to know the answer to her question of the night before. All night long it had tormented her. She had interpreted Alex's fury a thousand ways. She leant forward, 'I must know whether . . .'

Alex interrupted her with a gentle smile,

'No. I haven't made love to your daughter . . .'

'Thank God.'

'. . . yet.'

Lucy ignored the 'yet'. 'Thank God,' she said again and the lunch seemed bearable all at once. She even looked forward to the prospect of succulent lobster. She would just have this one lunch with him and then never see him again.

Alex saw her expression relax and felt an uncontrollable need to have her hanging on his words again. Anything was better than inattention. Dislike was better. Hatred was better. So great was his obsessional love that it could stand anything but indifference. He narrowed his eyes slightly.

'She longs to make love,' he said. 'I expect we shall very soon.'

'What?' said Lucy dimly.

'I'll take her to my flat.'

'But I know now!' Lucy's tones rang out.

'She's in love with me.'

'She's a child.'

'She's very beautiful.'

Alex had not particularly thought this about Eliza before; he recognized she was pretty, attractive, young, modern; he did not think of her in terms of beauty. But he felt instinctively in his new cruelty that it was the way to rouse Lucy. He probed her soft nerves as her fork had

pierced the white flesh of the lobster. It was something
he would never have dreamt of doing before but now it
came to him with inspired ease.

'But you don't love her.'

'How will you dissuade her from me? What will you
tell her?' Alex leant forward and his eyes gleamed crazily.
'Will you tell her about us?' He paused and watched as
Lucy became vivid with fury.

'No!' she cried passionately. 'No!'

'Will you tell her about her friend then?'

'What do you want . . .? Is it money . . .?' Lucy looked
at him and for a moment his head was bent. 'But you don't
love her,' she said again.

'Why do you assume that?' He remained with his head
low, he was debating within himself whether to declare
all now. For he understood why he had played with
Eliza. But what if Lucy said no? How could he bear that?
Yet surely he had left her no choice? He looked at her and
spoke quietly, 'But of course you're right . . . Lucy?'

Lucy looked down at her lobster and its claws and tail
seemed horribly ugly. She had the dreadful unaccustomed
feeling that she was losing a battle.

'Give me your hand, Lucy.' Half mesmerized she
stretched her right hand across the table. 'No. The other
one.'

Alex looked at the twisted gold wedding ring on her
finger and then carefully slid it off. 'All I ever wanted was
to be with you,' he said.

'Oh.' Lucy let her hand lie in his for she saw there was
nothing more she could do or say.

'We'll go for a walk,' said Alex gently, 'on Hampstead
Heath. It's a beautiful day. Cold but fresh. Bright and
beautiful.'

'I can't.' Dully, Lucy drew her coat round herself and,

as she felt Alex's eyes heavy on her, she added, 'I've got an appointment.'

'An appointment?'

'I can't today.' She stood up blunderingly and a waiter rushed to pull the table away.

'You enjoyed your lunch, yes?' His teeth were dazzling. Lucy blinked and yet her social manner replied for her.

'Yes. Very nice.'

'It was more than that,' said Alex as the waiter stood politely by. 'It was an event,' he put his hand on Lucy's shoulder. 'A new beginning. Not today. There's no hurry. No need for you to break an appointment. But tomorrow and tomorrow and tomorrow . . .'

'Ah. I'm late,' she murmured.

'We see you both again soon?' The patron bowed them out.

'Of course. Of course.' At last a triumphant smile broke through Alex's unreal calm.

They stood together on a pavement in Bond Street. It was busy with the end of lunchtime. The light was cruelly harsh after the dimly lit restaurant.

'Leave me now,' said Lucy, shading her eyes wearily. 'Leave me, please.'

But first he had to celebrate possession with a kiss. The agony of it. Lucy was horrified by the insistent pressure of his moist lips. It was horrifying to think she had once welcomed them. But it was worth submitting to watch him walk away and disappear into the crowds of people and cars. Now she walked herself, the appointment which had been true enough forgotten. And gradually the colour rose in her face, and her body which had been deadened by his presence became alive and warm. Then she became like a mad woman. She wanted to shout of Alex's perfidy to everyone she met. But who could she tell? Where could she go? Her house which in moments of distress usually provided her with a luxurious cocoon, she now imagined filled with Eliza's web of romantic imaginings. She could not face her daughter's youthful complacency – not yet. Most of all she wanted to speak to someone who would not need explanations, who would understand immediately the nightmare quality of the situation. Pushing her way along the crowded pavement, her eye was caught by a display window. She stopped abruptly. In her distraught state she didn't at first realize why, until she saw staring back at her a giant photograph of her own face. Calm, smiling, flatteringly shaded by garden greenery. She gazed bemusedly and finally realized she was standing outside the exhibition of Chloe's photographs. This was her appointment. Unconsciously, she had made her way towards it. The preview was that afternoon.

She started excitedly. Ah. What good fortune! Chloe would understand. Chloe would sympathize. Perhaps she would even have some idea of how to call Alex's bluff. That's all it was. Bluff. Hope made her eyes sparkle, her skin resume its usual lustre. Eagerly, she pushed open the heavy glass doors – and was met by a crowd of backs. But now she was all force and determination. Seeing Chloe among a group of admirers, she shouldered her way across and snatched her to one side.

'He's mad. Your brother's mad!'

Chloe stared. The selfishness of Lucy knew no bounds. At this moment of her triumph, limited perhaps, but triumph nevertheless, Lucy paraded her personal burden of misery. Of course she knew at once that Lucy had found out.

'I warned you he cut off my mouse's tail.' She turned from Lucy and fixed her eyes on a photograph of a laughing nun.

'But listen,' said Lucy and then paused. Her vitality now that she had captured Chloe seemed to slip away. Her face became stiff and weary. 'You've never been a mother,' she said eventually.

Chloe looked sad. Even in this moment of apparent tragedy Lucy had more to be happy about than she did. 'No. Unfortunately.'

Lucy put out her hand. 'I'm sorry, Chloe, I won't spoil your fun. I just thought you might be able to say something to him. I mean knowing him since he was a baby ...' Her voice died away as Chloe took her arm and placed her in front of a photograph. It was the same portrait of herself that she had seen in the window. The smooth smile stared back at her in huge pink close-up. Her face looked completely meaningless to her. As bland as blanc-mange and yet she supposed it would be admired as her face always was. For the first time her own beauty left her absolutely cold.

Chloe looked with her and then said slowly, 'You see, he really loves you, Lucy. Passionately. And it makes him forget how to behave.' Chloe could say no more. For all her affection and admiration for Lucy, she did not see how her brother's fatalistic love could be blocked. Some-times she felt herself becoming more of a camera than a human being and they were the moments when she felt most happy. She had been feeling like this when Lucy, so self-centredly distraught, had burst into her world of pictures. And now she found herself more able to wonder at the exaggeration of her brother's love than sympathize with Lucy. Lucy dealt in grand gestures; she should be able to appreciate what a great tribute Alex paid her. As for Eliza's fate – Lucy was right – she was not a mother. She could not understand why Eliza merited more protec-tion than any other girl. All girls suffered with thwarted love; she, Chloe, suffered with thwarted love most of the time. Nervously she turned away from the hard shiny blue eyes of Lucy's photograph. Lucy had put herself above other lesser mortals so she must accept that they could not reach up to help.

'You're cruel.' Lucy was still looking at her own face.

'Cruel?'

'Your photograph of me.'

'Everyone admires it.'

'You took it in my garden that autumn two years ago when I was so happy.'

'Yes. Everyone says that you look so . . .'

'Beautiful.' Lucy laughed, and instead of the usual soft tinkle it was a shrill and unattractive sound.

'Yes,' Chloe agreed and seemed about to go, but then added quietly, 'You might like my photograph of Eliza better.'

'What?'

'A photograph of Eliza.' In an oddly gentle manner Chloe took Lucy's arm and pushed the two of them across the crowded room. 'There.'

'Ah.' Lucy sighed. Chloe was right. She liked this picture more. Eliza didn't look beautiful. She didn't look special. She almost looked silly – with her wild hair and staring naïvety. But she did look like a human being. 'It's very good of her, Chloe. And I see you do understand what I'm protecting.'

'Yes. But I can't do anything about it.'

'No.' Lucy passed her hand over her face which seemed to set it in the lines of a sad madonna. 'And you say everyone thinks that my photograph is beautiful?'

'That *you* are beautiful!'

*

Lucy decided to tell Tom. It was inevitable, of course. She didn't know why she hadn't gone to him first. He was deeply protective of Eliza and believed, above all, in the importance of an innocent, unblemished childhood. The revelations necessary to change Eliza's love for Alex into revulsion would seem as impossible to him as they did to her.

Tom sat on the edge of her bed; although it was early in the morning, he was dressed and ready to leave. His face looked tired but as he watched his wife it filled with his usual loving admiration. Lucy wore a white wrap trimmed with swansdown. When she spoke, it beat wildly against her face. A posy of rich-coloured violets stood on her bedside table and surrounded her in a delicate fragrance. Leo had flown them back from a commercials job in South Africa.

Tom patted her soft hand.

'Darling. Are you really mother of three?'

Lucy, who hated disrupting beautiful scenes, particularly those in which she played the central part, knew she must hesitate no longer.

'Alex is Eliza's boyfriend,' she announced, despising any roundabout approach.

Tom did not remove his hand.

'Yes. I know.'

'What?'

'Though I'm afraid she didn't tell me herself. Eliza has more independence than I thought.'

'Tom!'

'Independence is generally considered a virtue.'

'Alex. She's going out with Alex!' Lucy hissed. She tried to clutch the tendrils of wavering swansdown; she felt them brushing her skin like Medusa's snakes.

'I would have stopped it if I could.'

'What shall we do? What shall we do?' Lucy cried out against her husband's calm. She could not believe this insane conversation was taking place in her fairyland bedroom, usually so full of sunshine and love. Tom actually seemed to be accepting the situation. Didn't he realize the danger?

Tom said calmly, 'She's very young. It can't be serious. She'll tire of him in a matter of weeks.'

Lucy had always relied on her husband's tolerant understanding to smooth over her passions. Didn't he understand that Eliza was a child, perhaps in one way, but a woman also? As Alex had said himself, a true daughter of Lucy's. Alex was not a dress to be worn for the winter and then thrown away. Besides, where would she find a man as charming as Alex? As clever. As handsome. As completely perfect. With despair Lucy realized afresh that she had herself created the man for Eliza's love. She might as well have commanded Eliza to fall in love with him.

'She won't fall out of love with him,' she said dismally. 'She thinks he's perfect. I told her that.'

Tom looked up sharply, 'I see. I see. Well, tell her you were wrong.'

'She wouldn't believe me. Why should she? Her views were fixed at a much more impressionable age.'

'Alex won't tell her about Jessie. He wouldn't do that.'

'I suppose not. But ...' Lucy paused and discovered that Tom's understanding had its limits. She could not tell him about Alex sliding off her wedding ring. She couldn't bring herself to tell him what Alex really wanted.

'Perhaps you should take him back,' said Tom quietly. 'And unmake him.'

'Oh,' Lucy gasped and had the sensation that she was drowning. That her husband should suggest such a thing. The thought of losing herself in Alex's burning black eyes filled her with horror. She felt the room had become dark and icy cold. 'I can't,' she whispered.

'No,' said Tom in a matter of fact voice. 'Well, I expect Eliza will grow out of it. Children are so resilient. And you know that girl Jessie really asked for it. I've every confidence in Eliza's basic good sense.' He bent down and picked up his brief-case. 'I think she's always been the hero-worshipping sort. Though, really, our best bet's that he'll tire of her. After all, she's awfully young for him.'

'Not as young as I am for you.'

'Well, yes. Still . . .' Tom leant forward and kissed Lucy's pale cheek in his usual affectionate manner. 'I must be off now, darling.'

'No. Tom . . .!' He had never failed her before. He could not mean to leave her.

'We'll talk more tonight.'

'What more is there to say?' Lucy watched hopelessly as he crossed her flowery carpet and disappeared through the white panelled door.

*

Lucy lay in the bath and the only words that remained with her from her conversation with Tom were his: 'Perhaps you should take him back and unmake him.' What else was there left for her to do? And yet how could she do that?

The water was cooling around her body; the flimsy soap bubbles dissolving and revealing her tired flesh. Today she felt old. Today she was supposed to be meeting Leo. Some people, she thought, felt their life enhanced by sacrifice. A warm glow of virtue quickened their blood. That was not for her.

With a feeling of nostalgia that made her realize she had already taken the decision, she pictured the simple enthusiasm and gaiety of Leo. Chloe was wrong. Alex did not love her. He was obsessed by her perhaps, but he did not love her. Love was a bright creative thing. Leo loved her. And today she must turn him off. Slowly she stepped out of the bath, and winding herself in a large towel, sat on the small cane chair which Eliza liked.

Alex's feelings for her were a destructive force. She remembered the priest that Eliza had admired in church who had spoken about the blood of the lamb turning to Coca-Cola. That was the morning Alex had seduced poor Jessie. Oh God! Lucy tried to pray. In order to avoid praying for herself she concentrated all her thoughts on Eliza and gradually she began to feel a kind of numbed calmness take over her limbs and brain. There was nothing else for it. She must receive Alex back and paint him for Eliza in new unattractive colours. The very fact of his turning to her mother (although she must see nothing more than admiration) would start the horrid process.

How ugly it all is, thought Lucy. So dead and ugly. She stood up and, finding herself quite dry now, let the towel fall to the ground. Immediately she was confronted by her naked body reflected in the long mirror opposite. Morning sun which had just started through the lace-shrouded window flecked her skin with gold. She un-pinned her hair so that it fell in massive curls around her shoulders. She thought she looked like some strange spotted animal, some wild jungloid beast. Luxurious, dangerous ... Lucy bared her teeth in a snarl and then, smiling at herself, raised her arms so that her breasts lifted and each nipple was ornamented by a golden medallion of light.

She had never been one to relish indecision. This was what distinguished her from most women and made her so much stronger. Now she had decided to take Alex back, her old ebullience began to reassert itself and already she was planning how to make it all less odious, how to coat the pill with sugar. Moving swiftly, she entered the bedroom and picked from her wardrobe a cream silk suit with a sapphire blue velvet waistcoat and high blue suede boots. Poor Leo. Poor Leo. As the virtuous wife she would cast him off. Not that she really expected or wanted him to suffer; he was too full of life for that. She sighed for a moment, but then swept a brush through her hair in stern resolve.

As the virtuous mother she would accept Alex back.

It was nearly Christmas and they would be going to Scotland in a few days. She would invite him to stay. And Chloe, despite her perfidy, and as many other talented and beautiful people as could be fitted into the house. Perhaps even Leo just for a day or two. No. Regretfully, she abandoned that idea. But still, there was hope in plans like these. There was a future ahead.

8

Lucy triumphantly succeeded in gathering together a
Scottish house party. There were Philippa and Teddy
Verney-Smith who graced every guest list – she so jolly
and well-connected, he so cheerful and rich; there was
Chloe; there was Chloe's friend, Reynolds, who wrote
every article anyone read on antiques but was otherwise
a bit of a dark horse; there were Nadia and Edward
Cavalier, who so doted on each other and owned such big
estates in the Burgundy district; and there was Harrison
who was something very important in New York but had
not yet been properly discovered in England. Lucy prided
herself in compiling an interesting mixture of the old and
the new, the known and the unknown. She laid in food
enough for an army and drink enough for a drunken army.
The organizational challenge went some way to improving
her state of mind, till she began the actual allocation of
bedrooms. Tom's room was to her left and to her right
there was another. It always belonged to her lover. Alex
must have it. The thought of his presence, so close to her
for every night they were there, filled her with oppressive
foreboding. However it must be done.

Eliza was in an ecstasy of anticipation. Alex filled her
thoughts and in her romantic imagination together they
roamed the windy moors. She saw herself as Cathy and
him as Heathcliff; together they would discover the very
heart of nature, of God and of their love for each other.
Alex had never mentioned the word love to her, but so
great was her emotion that she needed no reassurance

from him. Scotland had been her childhood playground and now it would be the scene of her growing up.

Alex himself, in the few days before they went north, was curiously elusive. Neither mother nor daughter saw him as much as they expected. One with heartfelt relief and the other with some vague feeling that he was preparing for the great adventure that was before them. Like a bride, Eliza felt they should not meet before.

In a way she was close to the truth except that Alex was waiting to have Lucy again. It seemed right to him that Scotland, where they had been most united before, should be the scene for the rebirth of their relationship. When Eliza had given him the invitation he had known at once what it signified, who it had really come from. He passed the days half-dazed and when Chloe rang up, he found her surprise that he, too, should be going up to Scotland quite incomprehensible. 'But of course, I'm staying with them,' he said. 'Lucy asked me. She wants me particularly.'

'Lucy?' said Chloe ironically.

'Lucy,' repeated Alex with childlike reverence.

'Oh well,' said Chloe and decided to be selfish for once. No doubt Lucy had some plan afoot and she would hear of it soon enough. Meanwhile, she was looking forward to a change from the limited pleasures of her London flat to the luxury of Lucy's *modus vivendi*. She had hopes, too, of Reynolds, who was not only intelligent, amusing and successful, but also (unique in her experience) unmarried. Let her passionate brother and her super friend work out their own problems.

Tom accepted the news of Alex becoming one of their party with perfect equanimity, so that Lucy decided he had known all along she would follow his advice. But she didn't reopen the subject. Her only wish was to get the whole matter settled with as little ugliness as possible. This was why she was throwing such a social spangled veil over their Scottish house. If the house was a pleasure dome, the countryside a magnificent wilderness, the people beautiful and talented, the entertainment splendid, surely nothing ugly could take place there?

Unfortunately for Lucy's plans, Alex noticed nothing about Scotland except that it was where he and Lucy had made such orgiastic love. He didn't notice the other people. He didn't notice the champagne flowing or the superb venison. He gazed at Lucy with avid eyes until Eliza said to him wonderingly, 'You're so strange, Alex. Are you feeling ill?' And then he made an effort to behave more normally.

On the first afternoon the whole party went out into cold pine-smelling air for a reviving walk.

'Tomorrow, I've arranged a picnic,' announced Lucy whose indomitable spirits had always risen far above such ordinary discomforts as cold.

'A picnic!' shrieked Philippa, who responded energetically to every suggestion. 'In this weather?'

'I wouldn't put it past Lucy to go for a swim,' mocked Teddy.

Lucy smiled, accepting their horror as a compliment. 'We'll have the picnic in a shooting lodge and afterwards go for a really long walk. Up the mountainside.'

'The lazy ones can sit in front of a fire and read the newspapers,' said Tom kindly.

'Perfect.'

'Excellent.' Nadia and Edward pledged a comfortable afternoon in each other's company.

'Do you remember the hunting lodge?' Eliza asked Alex a little shyly, for she realized the associations here must mean more to her than to him.

'Very well.' Alex looked down at her vaguely. He had not been aware of her presence at his side. Lucy's voice, now lecturing Harrison on Scottish castles, rang in his ears.

'Do you really remember it?' Eliza insisted, obscurely pleased.

'Below it is the loch where Lucy always swims.'

'We all do,' Eliza reacted quickly against her exclusion from his memory.

'Yes,' agreed Alex, not noticing he had upset her. The idea of the picnic in that particular place filled him with excitement. One summer's day after lunch when Tom was lying on the turf reading his *Financial Times* and the children were playing somewhere by the loch, Lucy and he had climbed up to the lodge and found an old iron bedstead in one of the musty rooms. He had watched the faded and peeling wallpaper as they had made love. It had been a pattern of blackberries on a trellis-work of leaves. He could have drawn it still.

*

That evening Lucy was more dazzling than ever. She was dressed all in gold, from a heavy necklace round her white throat to gold-embroidered slippers on her bare feet. The drawing-room was very warm; an enormous fire blazed in the hearth. A glowing Christmas tree stood in a wide bow window. On every chair or stool or cushion lounged a brilliantly clad woman or a man in evening dress. Yet their attitude was relaxed and casual. Except for Eliza.

Eliza felt uneasy, as if she might stifle in the luxurious atmosphere. It was the first time she had ever stayed up for dinner in Scotland and the consciousness of this made her nervous which increased her heat. Also, she was wearing a long woollen skirt, a cast-off of Lucy's, which had seemed beautiful up in her bedroom but down here among the glittering silks seemed heavy and unfeminine. Nevertheless when Alex was placed beside her at the dinner table, she managed to tell herself how unimportant were clothes and appearance. It was the spirit that mattered. She did not notice Lucy's white hand with its shining rings and pearly nails linger around Alex's shoulder as she pointed him to his seat. She did not see her mother's wide pink lips purse as if to kiss.

Chloe noticed and wondered. She turned to Reynolds who was studying his crystal glass,

'Would you say Lucy was perfection?'

He looked down the table through the sparkling glass and then smiled at her.

'"What's come to perfection perishes."'

Chloe decided he had an interesting face with that heavy nose and light-coloured eyes. She might ask to photograph him.

'Browning's one of my favourite poets.'

Eliza was feeling much better after a glass or two of red wine. And Alex had become quite cheerful and attentive. He was ragging her about the number of exams she was taking.

'Why does a pretty girl like you want to have all those letters after her name? All these O Levels and then all those A Levels and S Levels, and then University and B.A. and M.A. and D.Litt. and D.Phil.'

'Oh, but I won't get them all,' Eliza protested, for she couldn't help taking seriously anything he said.

'Worse still. Much worse. Haven't you heard "A little learning is a dangerous thing"?'

'"Drink deep or taste not the Pierian spring."' Proudly she completed the quotation.

'There you are then; you agree with me. Much nicer to be a wild wood nymph.'

'Oh, yes,' agreed Eliza, his words finding an echo in her memory, 'I'm longing for the walk and picnic tomorrow!'

After dinner was finished, Lucy was filled with even more energy than usual. She had noticed Alex's playful manner and Eliza's flushed excited cheeks and blamed herself for letting the situation develop. She had thought it would be enough to hint to Alex that her favours would come.

'Let's play charades!' she cried the moment coffee had disappeared. 'Tom and I shall choose teams.' And before any protests could register against such a glorious commander, half the party found themselves outside the drawing-room door. Among them was Alex and not among them was Eliza.

'We must have costumes,' exclaimed Philippa.

'Oh, yes.' Lucy took Alex's arm. 'We'll find some upstairs. You think of a word.'

'In-say-she-a-bull.' Reynolds' suggestion followed them up the stairs.

Lucy turned off the wide oak stairs to a narrower corridor which led to the children's part of the house.

'There's a dressing-up box in the nursery,' she said over her shoulder to Alex. He came level with her in the dimly lit corridor and pulled her towards him. Although Lucy had engineered it, she was horribly reluctant. For the first time in her life she felt debauched. She had never before given or received a caress, unless carried away on a wave of romantic desire.

But Alex felt nothing missing. He sighed heavily as he let her go.

'Ah, Lucy. Lucy. My darling Lucy.' His sensations were so acute that he could trace the embroidered pattern of her dress with his finger tips. He put his fingers round her warm neck and the softness and closeness of her overwhelmed him.

'We mustn't be too long,' said Lucy. They wandered to the nursery both savouring in silence the after-taste of their kiss. For different reasons they had both fallen into a kind of numbness. Alex wanted to preserve for ever the feeling of her skin and Lucy wanted to dull all feelings whatever.

The nanny was watching television in the nursery. Her eyes widened at the vision that Lucy's golden glory presented in the drab room. Obligingly she pulled out the dressing-up box and began to tug out the contents.

'There you are, Mrs Trevelyan. That's all the best stuff.'

Alex was piled high with velvet feathered hats, sequined boleros, a busby, swords, capes, furs, breeches, a riding hat, a hussar's uniform. Lucy followed behind, dangling a selection of masks from her arms. In an unconscious act of self-defence she placed one, a black cat with scarlet nose and emerald eyes, over her own face.

'Ah!' gasped Alex turning to her just before they reached the main staircase.

'Tomorrow,' whispered the black cat and the sable whiskers quivered. 'Not tonight. Tomorrow.'

'Lucy, my darling.' Alex could say or do no more, for his arms were balancing the sliding clothes, but he had accepted what she said. Tomorrow they were going up to the shooting lodge.

*

The next day was Sunday so the local Catholic church had to be visited before any revelry could begin. The party became divided into believers and non-believers, the latter proceeding as an advance group up to the shooting lodge. Alex decided to attend Mass.

Eliza was filled with delight. She had woken up with odd sensations about the night before which her hot and buzzing head, a legacy from too much champagne and red wine, did not help to clarify. She felt that Alex had not been wholly attentive and yet she recalled his bantering affection at dinner. Perhaps it was just that they had played so many games and he had always been on the other side. But to go to church with him would restore everything. She felt sure he realized this.

Chloe, who was not a Catholic, also decided to go to church and was surprised when Reynolds joined her. He was turning out to be a man of surprises.

'But I happen to be a Catholic,' he protested when she challenged him.

So two cars went down the little valley to the stone church. Lucy, annoyed by this turn-out, larger than she had bargained for, made sure that her family filled the whole length of one pew. Nevertheless she couldn't help but be aware of Alex's tall figure behind her and Chloe's girlish but similar profile and that clever young man with his odd pale eyes. Under any other circumstances she might have been more than interested in him.

Lucy was right to sense Alex's gaze on her. He watched her like a bird watches its prey. He had no doubt that she would keep her word and he was in a state of excited anticipation. When the bell was rung and Lucy left her pew to take communion at the altar rails, he only just stopped himself following her. When she returned with eyes cast humbly down, he saw nothing but the shape of her mouth, so that Eliza who followed by, in her self-consciousness sure he was watching her, could have been anyone at all.

'Well, what do you faithless creatures think of the real

thing?' Tom stood in the church's porch and slapped Alex's shoulder. He seemed in jovial mood.

'I shan't judge till Christmas Day,' said Chloe. 'That's when they pull out all the stops.'

'I love the smell of that church,' said Lucy, 'the musty holiness of it. You know we had Eliza baptized there.'

Eliza looked startled as an image of herself in flowing robes was put before them. Her leather tasselled skirt seemed to lose some of its sophisticate's significance.

'I'll drive,' offered Alex, who felt a sudden need for action. Lucy put her arm through his,

'We'll take Chloe and Reynolds in the little car. Leave poor Tom to cope with the children.'

'Come on, Lizzie,' Tom gripped Eliza who was standing dimly staring, 'it's not the first time we've been used as nannies.'

*

As they wound up from valley to mountainside, the day which had been cold but promising better with sudden bursts of sunshine, became set in a heavy grey. A wind, which had hardly been noticeable lower down, blustered around the car and flung across the barren landscape.

'Not very inviting, is it?' said Chloe, who was usually forgiven such remarks.

'Don't be so feeble.' Lucy turned from the front seat angrily and then, hearing her own ugly tones, pointed ahead. 'Look, you can see the smoke coming from the lodge's chimney. They'll have an enormous fire going by now. A bit of the alternative water of life and it'll seem like the Ritz.'

Sure enough the white fluttering smoke was clearly visible above the rising heather and soon they turned the corner into full view of the house.

'Holloa!' Philippa, stoutly clad in fur boots and duffle

coat, waved at them from the door. The *Sunday Express* poked out from under her arm.

'The newspapers. How very civilized,' commented Reynolds agreeably.

Inside the house the scene was more disorganized, for the picnic baskets, unloaded but not unpacked by Lucy's pampered guests, lay around the floors and chairs.

'But you haven't even opened the whisky,' cried Lucy. 'What an abstemious lot.'

'We hadn't the benefit of your holy thirst.' Teddy took a pile of mugs from Lucy's outstretched hand.

Alex stayed outside the house for a moment, watching the thick clouds cross behind the mountainside. He looked forward to climbing its ragged slopes after lunch and peering down on the rest of the world. He turned to go in just as the second car with Tom at its wheel came up the flinty track. Immediately it stopped, Eliza jumped out and ran towards him. Her hair blew about her face.

'Isn't it glorious up here! So fierce and free. I don't know how one ever lives in London.'

Alex smiled at her enthusiasm and put out his hand to catch her hair. She twisted away from him, eyes flashing.

'You're like a highland pony.' Alex laughed at her wildness. She did indeed remind him of one of those stray colts one admires from a car window and then forgets a moment later. Eliza was not altogether pleased by the analogy and with a fussy embarrassed gesture ran over to collect Ticky who was trying to scramble up the mountain. When she returned, Alex had disappeared inside the house.

Lunch was a raving success of lamb cutlets, scotch eggs, smoked salmon, turkey pie, cherry tarts, stilton and much too good red wine.

'Darling, but it's '59.'

'Tom's so generous.' Lucy looked vague. She had settled

at last on a tattered cushion beside the fire and her face glowed in its flames. Above her, Alex had taken the corner of the sofa so his long legs supported her back.

'It's specially chosen to give us strength for the great climb,' said Tom. He was standing by the bow window, eating a large sandwich of bread and cheese. Sometimes he seemed to be remote from the room and only concerned with watching the clouds and heather outside the window and at other times his whole attention seemed to be focused on the hearth. When he looked at Lucy, a curious mixture of admiration and pity crossed his face.

Eliza wandered round the room, too self-conscious to settle. She picked up a newspaper when someone else did and put it down when they put theirs down. Her wild happiness was turning into a frustrated restlessness. She listened to the grown-ups talking about the news and could not join in on the proper negligent level.

'Come on, Eliza,' said Chloe, taking pity on her, 'come and join us here.' Chloe and Reynolds and Harrison, whose appreciation of being part of such an un-American scene did not stop him from delivering a well-informed but misplaced lecture on 'bussing', had found a table for themselves.

'No,' Eliza was grateful really, but could not bear the confinement of such a small circle, 'no, I'm going outside to play football with Rupert.'

The finishing of lunch with Irish coffee coincided with a brightening in the sky, but even so Tom's suggestion that they took some air met with a marked lack of response. In the end Chloe, Lucy and Alex were persuaded outside.

'Brrhhh.' Chloe swung her arms. 'We must all be mad.'

'Wait for me,' called Eliza, as they started up the low granite slopes.

Lucy climbed ahead. Her long legs in their scarlet

ribbed tights pushed impatiently against her knee-length skirt. She thought it irreverent to wear trousers in church. Alex kept up with her. His energy, the product of excitement and good humour, was such that he could have run ahead and pulled her up behind him but he liked staying at her elbow and catching the occasional look she threw over her shoulder.

'Whew!' said Tom, after a bit of this. And he sat down on a boulder. 'I'm not sure I trust my heart.' They all stopped and the wind blew them into profile on the barren mountain side. Chloe collapsed onto another boulder.

Alex laughed. He pointed further up to where the track divided into two, one track going straight up to the top and the other winding more gently round the side and up behind. 'Let's have a race. We'll split. Try the two routes.'

'Yes!' cried Eliza eagerly. 'And make the shepherd's hut at the top the winning post.'

'One's steep and short and the other's longer and less of a climb.'

'No.' Tom raised his hand. 'I'm taking no part of it. At my time of life I have every right to potter back and entertain our other guests.'

'They'll probably have gone already,' said Lucy in some kind of appeal.

'Then I shall look into the glowing embers.'

'I'm for the short road.' Chloe rose waveringly to her feet.

'Right,' Alex responded immediately by taking Lucy's arm. 'You and Eliza take the short and narrow route and we two oldies will take the primrose path.'

'Oh,' Eliza wasn't able to hide her disappointment, but she didn't know how to object without appearing childish.

'Come on,' said Chloe, as she stood indecisively. 'You've heard of the tortoise and the hare.'

Tom sat on his boulder and watched until the four figures had divided and set out along their separate paths. He thought how quickly human beings became small and insignificant dots against such large landscape. Then, the cold wind becoming too much for even his Highland tweed coat, he started slowly down the hill.

Eliza was determined to get to the hut first. The urge to win made her hector poor Chloe, who only wanted a post-prandial stroll.

'But you don't think Alex and your mother will be running along like this, do you?' she asked eventually.

'It's a race,' Eliza strode on stubbornly.

Chloe was quite right. Now that Alex had Lucy to himself, all his urge for action or at least any action that might separate them had left him. He took her arm and helped her along the narrow winding path.

'It's not really made for two,' said Lucy, trying to smile.

'It's made by sheep for sheep,' said Alex. 'Are you tired?'

'No. No. Not really.'

They went on a little further in silence till they reached a stone wall. Very carefully, Alex handed Lucy up to it and then jumped her down the other side. When her feet touched the ground he didn't let go of her. 'Let's sit down a moment,' he said, and before she could object he took off his macintosh and laid it alongside the piled stones. It was oddly cosy in the lee of the wall for the wind sailed straight over it and left them in a quiet space of their own.

Lucy felt the same kind of numbness coming over her limbs as had the night before, after Alex's kiss. This time it was even more deadening, for the combination of the drink at lunch and the ice-cold walk had dazed her body.

Alex put his arm around her body and pulled her to him. For a moment he was content to lie with her but soon the warmth of her body which came to him sweetly through her heavy coat and the smell of the scent she always wore began to rouse him further. He put his hand on her legs and the feeling of the wool under his fingers gave him a sensuous longing to feel the real silky body that was underneath. He slid his hand up her leg and under her skirt and when he found warm flesh around her hips, he shuddered.

Such was his ecstasy that he didn't wonder at Lucy's silence. He didn't question that their making love which had always been so natural and unashamedly eager should have become so silent. Then Lucy said,

'We can't here. Anyone might see us.'

But it was too late. Alex was panting. She felt his hot breath in her face, around her ears. 'You love it outside. You always have. You love it where anyone can see. You know you do.'

'Ah,' Lucy gasped as she felt his weight about to submerge her, and yet that was better than feeling each separate act of his. For no one had ever taken her against her will before and it was as if each part of her was submitting in turn to his superior power. It was better to lose herself all at once. Yet she again tried to stop him and already she was willing to sacrifice her daughter.

'Eliza,' she whispered, finding nothing else to say but the name, 'Eliza.' But Alex didn't even hear. His head and body was filled with Lucy. The two years between the time when he had last had her in this way was a vacant space that must be filled.

*

Eliza flung herself up the last and steepest stretch of the mountain, 'I can see it! I can see it!' she cried to Chloe who was struggling along behind.

'I expect you can,' murmured Chloe. She reached the top herself and watched as Eliza ran on to the hut which was a few yards across the flat plateau top. She disappeared inside only to pop out again in a second.

'We've won! We've won. They're not here yet. There's nobody here but us.'

'That's no surprise to me,' Chloe shouted back at her. 'Now go away and play, dear, while I die quietly.' She collapsed onto the short turf which had taken over from the heather and slag.

Eliza went round the back of the hut, as if to make sure Alex and Lucy weren't hiding, and finally came and joined the prostrate Chloe,

'Mummy's an awfully fast walker, you know.'

'Perhaps her mind wasn't on the race.'

'Oh, she's very competitive.'

'Not as much as someone I know.' Chloe sat up and hugged herself. 'I have a feeling that when I stop being unbearably hot I'm going to be unbearably cold. I hope they hurry up.'

*

Lucy lay with wide open eyes and the shapes of the grey stones in the wall made an extraordinary pattern. She began to think of a new design for a wallpaper and managed for several minutes to forget where she was and what had just happened. Then she recalled why she was there. After all, the first time was certain to be the worst. Already Eliza was feeling put out by Alex's lack of attention. And then a tear appeared on her cheek. She felt so sullied, despoiled, destroyed by Alex. She didn't know how she could go on.

Alex was smiling. He had never felt Lucy so much part of him. In the past he had wanted to start making love all over again the moment they had finished, because almost at once she seemed to disappear from him back into the self-sufficiency he couldn't reach. But this time she had felt so quiescent, so submitting. He yawned and stretched, not noticing the ice-cold draught this caused between their two bodies. He had never felt so content.

Lucy shivered and huddled deeper. She shut her eyes again and then unable to stop her thoughts said drearily, 'They'll be waiting for us.'

'Oh, they'll think we've given up.'

*

Chloe stood up and stamped her feet,

'Sorry, Eliza. It's home for me.'

'Don't be such a spoil-sport. They'll be here any minute.'

'For one thing, it's about to rain.'

'We can go into the hut.' Desperately she ran into the low doorway. 'It's lovely and warm.'

'And smells of sheep dung and shepherd's pee. No thanks. I prefer whisky and a hot bath.'

'But ...' Eliza strained her eyes down the hillside. 'They'll wonder what has happened to us.'

'I doubt that.' Chloe turned her back firmly. 'That was a definite spot of rain.' And she started back.

'Oh,' Eliza was almost in tears; she hovered indecisively; why had this day she had been looking forward to so much turned out so horridly? 'All right. Wait for me. I'm coming.'

*

With great reluctance, Alex was forced to admit that it was raining. He moved Lucy gently, so he could see her face.

'Darling. It's raining.'

'Ah.' Lucy would have reacted no more if he'd said there was a tidal wave about to engulf them.

'We'd better go down.' He helped her to her feet and as he brushed down her skirt, she thought that she felt as if she'd known that wall all her life. They climbed over it and started back.

Tom had found Lucy was right when he got back to the house and it was already deserted. He read a discarded newspaper, stoked up the fire and then went out again. He was restless, unable to maintain his usual calm exterior. He looked up at the mountainside several times, but could see nothing move on its black surface. When it started to rain, he returned to the house and found an old black plastic macintosh. With this rolled up under his arm, he walked to the base of the mountain again. Almost at once he saw the two couples coming down their separate tracks. They couldn't see each other yet. Alex and Lucy were slightly ahead and although moving slower would reach the ground first. He started out to meet them.

Lucy's hair and face were streaming with water. She had refused Alex's offer of his coat. She said she liked the feeling of its fresh purity but in fact the rain was disguising her tears. Alex accepted her word and himself enjoyed the ice-cold fountain which was so majestically removed from London showers of dirt. Quite soon he saw Tom. His good humour extended particularly to Lucy's husband.

'Look,' he said happily, 'here's Tom come to meet us.' Lucy peered down through spiky clinging lashes.

'Yes,' she said dully. 'He's come to meet us.'

Tom unrolled the macintosh as he reached them and placed it right over Lucy's head and body so that she looked like a woman in deep mourning. Then he put his arm round her shoulders and led her down. Alex followed silently, keeping close to himself his sense of contentment. Just before they reached the bottom, there was a shout above the beating rain.

'Alex! Alex! Mummy!' Eliza came sliding down behind them. Tom took no notice and continued on with Lucy to the shooting lodge.

'Gosh,' said Eliza, who had at least partially recovered her spirits with the soaking and exercise. 'I'm sodden. Where ever were you? We waited ages.'

'And you're not even a St Bernard,' said Chloe joining them. She looked at Alex as closely as the pouring rain would let her. She seemed to take note of something there and then continued impatiently, 'Come on. Don't just stand there. This isn't Trafalgar Square. I'll bet that angel Tom's got something to warm our cockles.'

9

That evening, Lucy lay across her bed as if asleep. She hadn't bothered to brush her hair since the rain, and it lay in matted tangles round her shoulders. Her cheeks were flushed and she breathed heavily.

Tom came into the room. He was ready dressed for dinner except that he had not yet put on his jacket.

'Are you ill?' he said gently.

Lucy didn't answer for a while and then said flatly, 'You know.'

Tom came and sat on the bed, and pushed her hair off her hot face. He didn't know what he could say to her, but the sight of her lying there in such misery was torture to him. His adoration for Lucy could not stand seeing her brought low in this way. It was as if someone had daubed a moustache on a painting of the madonna. It was shocking, unbearable. Almost obscene. He wanted desperately for her to be restored to herself. But what could he say?

He went over to her wardrobe and took out the silk kaftan which she had just had made.

'Put this on,' he said. 'Brush your hair. You'll feel better.'

Lucy sat up and the sight of the kaftan gave her some energy. 'I can't do it, Tom. I can't. He's a destroyer. He'll never let me go. He wants to destroy me.'

Tom looked at her. He could have said, 'We'll have to tell Eliza then. About Jessica. And about you.' But he didn't have to. Lucy saw it in his face and besides it was for ever in her head. She took the dress from his hands and walked wearily over to the bathroom door. 'I'll see you downstairs,' she said.

'I'll have a glass of champagne for you.' Tom watched her seriously and then added just before going out of the room. 'Eliza seems very downcast.'

Lucy met his look resignedly and then lifted her hands in an attitude of despair. Since Tom made no movement to her side she dropped them again and went into the bathroom.

*

Eliza was as far away as she could be from Alex at the dinner table. To her right was her father, to her left Reynolds. The latter rather frightened her because he was not as smooth-talking as the men who usually came to the house and she suspected he might say whatever came into his head. However, once she had realized Alex was too far away for any winning contact she decided to enjoy herself anyway. Her confidence which she had gained in France and which had been draining away as she found herself put once more in the position of a child, came obediently when she called. For she soon discovered that Reynolds, serious or not, was ready to take her seriously. In fact he seemed very keen to get her views on antique prices in Paris about which he was shortly to write an article. With growing enjoyment she discovered she was really rather well-informed.

Chloe, on Reynolds' other side, watched them and thought it would be too much if Lucy's daughter were to pip her at the post. There was no doubt that Eliza had inherited her mother's looks, although there was something more serenely classical and less frenetic about her dark beauty. She thought what a pity it was that Lucy had been born quite so clever. She would never be satisfied. She looked over the table to where her brother bent towards

Lucy. She understood now what Lucy was doing. Why she had invited Alex whom Chloe knew she could not bear to have in the same room as her. And it seemed she was succeeding. Chloe glanced sideways at Reynolds. Well, she supposed he was only her own little house-present for such lavish hospitality. She stared at Lucy through the flickering candlelight again and caught an odd pale reflection of her face. Suddenly she wondered whether Lucy had not made a terrible mistake. For how would she ever get rid of Alex now?

Lucy was thinking the same dreadful thought. It was as if the dark attentive man at her side was Satan and had bought her soul. How could she ever be free of him now? She could free Eliza of him easily enough. But how could she free herself? She turned to Teddy's fatuous face on her right and loved the affable ordinariness of him.

Tom sat at the other end of the table and tried to see his wife. But the two giant candelabra obscured her face, so that he could catch only the top of her glinting golden hair. And that, he knew was false, for she had piled her own tangled mass under a wig. He was so preoccupied that Philippa, a usually unnoticing girl, seated on his right found herself straining to see what he saw.

'Have another glass, m'dear,' seemed to be his only conversation.

After dinner Philippa took her revenge by insisting that they played bridge. In fact Tom rather enjoyed the game as he was a very good player, but since his marriage he generally deferred to Lucy's view of it which was that it was a totally unsociable, uncivilized way of passing an evening. However, this night she seemed relieved to find an easy occupation for her guests and only expressed any disagreement when it appeared Alex would not be included in the two tables.

'Tom, darling, you can't let poor Alex sit about. Let him take your place.' Tom looked across at Lucy whose face had changed from pallor to pink and whose manner from the languid to the agitated.

'Of course. Dreadful game. He's welcome.'

'But I only want to sit in homage at Lucy's feet,' Alex smiled, but such was his certainty that he didn't really mind being separated from her. Tom went over to Lucy,

'You don't look well, darling. Perhaps you caught a chill. It would be a pity to spoil Christmas.' He looked for a moment at the Christmas tree, at the glittering fairy on top. 'Why don't you go to bed? Eliza can take you up and settle you in.'

Hearing her name, Eliza turned round from her position at Reynolds' elbow; as a non-bridge-player, she was able to move from player to player. She was clearly reluctant to leave.

'No. No. Don't bother Eliza,' Lucy said hastily. 'Let's have a game of chess, the two of us, and then I'll go.'

So Lucy and Tom played chess on a little table beside the fire and were quite silent except for the end when they both said 'Check'. But as it turned out it was stalemate.

'I hate that,' said Lucy. 'Stalemate.' And she looked up to where the bridge fours were noisily debating the points. 'I'm to bed.' Without saying good night to anyone she slipped away.

Tom continued to sit by the fire and became half mesmerized by the glowing red and the occasional spurt of blue flame.

*

The party broke up after midnight with a good deal of noise. At the bottom of the stairs Tom put his hand on Alex's shoulder.

'Let's hope the rain clears tomorrow.'

'Early start, is it?'

'I like to be there at the beginning. Dundalk likes it.'

'Good host, is he?'

'Excellent. There's just us and Teddy from this house. I'll see you're called.'

'Make it a good loud knocking. Your hospitality's so good.' Alex smiled and as everyone disappeared upstairs to their rooms, he wandered back for a moment of peace to the drawing-room. There he found Eliza curled up in an armchair.

'Hey. Rather late for little girls.'

'I'm not little.' She stretched her arms sensuously above her head.

'No. No. I do see that.' He went over to the curtained window and pulled back a corner of the heavy material. 'There's a beautiful moon.'

'It's going to be a beautiful day tomorrow.'

'Every day here is.'

'Why don't you sit down?'

'It's late.'

'All the more reason for sitting down.' Alex looked at Eliza and even in his oblivious state, he couldn't help noticing her invitation. A slight feeling of regret tinged his self-satisfaction. He bent over her and carefully avoiding her clinging arms kissed her on the cheek,

'You're very sweet,' he said. 'And very young.'

'Oh,' Eliza pouted as he started to move away. 'You never talked so much about my age when we were in London.' But she was too sleepy and too contentedly conscious of her success in entering the adult world that evening to make much protest. 'I suppose I must go to bed too.' And this time her yawn was a genuine one of tiredness.

'Ah,' said Alex, now hesitating slightly. 'You can sleep your head off, it's the men that must be up and away.'

'The men?'

'The guns.'

'I'd forgotten. The shoot. Oh, how dull! You'll be away all day.'

10

It was three o'clock in the morning; that time of the night or early morning when death seems closer than life. Lucy's bedroom was black and yet a pair of eyes stared into it as if they could see. Tom had not slept that night and he didn't expect to before he got up. Lucy stirred in her sleep and he put a hand out to smooth her naked arm.

Earlier they had made love. It was like a continuation of their game of chess in the drawing-room, except this time they had come to an understanding. There was no stalemate. Lucy had trusted him. Had left it with him and now she had fallen into a calm sleep.

Tom lay awake. It was seldom now that he shared Lucy's bed. She didn't shut her door on him. They just didn't often do things together that led to them making love. She would have, of course, if he'd asked. So it was a rather special occasion to be lying awake with Lucy in his arms. But that was not why he stared into the darkness.

At about seven he eased his wrist from under Lucy's hair and looked at the luminous dial of the watch. Then he rolled her body gently from him and slid out of the bed. Naked, he went to the window and drew back the curtain, but the moon that Alex had admired from the drawing-room the night before had disappeared and no dawn had yet taken its place. The view was black and ghostly; a faint wind rattled a scattering of unswept pine needles. Shutting the curtain again, he went silently from the room and to his own bathroom. The old pipes thumped gently as he ran himself a bath and then sighed as he turned the taps off.

At eight there was only the slightest hint of light as Tom walked quietly from his room to Alex's. He knocked on the door. And then knocked again before he got a muffled response. He went once more to Lucy's bedroom and peered at her still smoothly sleeping face. He did not kiss her but, as if given a sense of urgency by the sight, he left the room briskly and went downstairs to where a flask of coffee stood on the hall table.

Alex and Teddy didn't join him until he was outside by the car. He was a shadowy figure in the misty dawn as he loaded the guns and cartridge bags into the back.

'Top o' the morning to you.' Teddy, his pink face striving for some determined shape, strode out from the house.

'Well, I hope so,' answered Tom vaguely. Alex appeared behind Teddy. His finely-cut smooth face looked young and vulnerable in the pallor of the early-morning light. He still held a cup of coffee in his hand,

'Early bird,' he said, pointing it at Tom.

'I like to see to the guns myself.'

'Very proper.' Teddy shivered and got into the car. 'Mustn't catch a chill.' Tom and Alex continued to stand outside the car, each staring at some faraway point among the dark pines and spruces that started spikily out of the skyline and continued downwards towards them in unshaven irregularity.

Upstairs in her warm bed Lucy moved and then quite suddenly pushed back the bedclothes and sprang out of bed. She ran across the room and pulled back a curtain.

'Ah,' she sighed and half let it fall. The large white estate car was moving slowly from the driveway. She could see the figures in it quite clearly and she watched till it rounded a bend and went out of sight. Then, 'Ah,' she sighed again and picking up her nightdress returned to the bed where she once more fell to sleep.

*

Eliza came quietly along the corridor to her mother's bedroom door. With some difficulty, since she was holding a breakfast tray, she turned the door handle. Her motives in being so apparently daughterly were actually rather mixed. She thought she was being kind and loving to her poor mother who hadn't been feeling at all well yesterday. But unconsciously she was eager to see Lucy in a less than dominating position. She was hoping for the patronage that comes with pity.

She laid the tray on the end of the bed and went to draw the curtains.

'Mummy,' she whispered. 'It's nearly ten o'clock.'

Lucy was more awake than she seemed but she was feeling so deliciously lazy. She had always appreciated that the other side of her tremendous energy was a tremendous need for relaxation.

'Ah, darling,' she said, putting out an arm. 'You are sweet to bring me my breakfast.'

Eliza was a little surprised by her light unruffled tone and did not alter her own voice of concern, 'It was probably getting so wet that made you feel awful. You must take it easy today.'

'Get me my brush, would you, darling,' Lucy sat up gracefully among the pillows. 'I do hate sticky hair.'

Obediently Eliza brought it from her dressing-table and then while Lucy energetically brushed out her tangles began to straighten her bed. 'The men went out early,' she said eventually. 'They can hardly have slept at all.'

'I slept marvellously,' Lucy yawned with catlike satisfaction and threw the brush to the end of the bed. 'And now I'm ravenous!'

Eliza pulled up the tray and then hesitated. She really hadn't expected a scene like this at all. 'It'll be awfully boring all day without them,' she said eventually.

'The Cavaliers are here, Philippa's here, Harrison's here and,' Lucy paused significantly, 'Reynolds's here.' She lifted a cup of steaming coffee with obvious satisfaction.

'Yes. I suppose so.' Eliza blushed slightly. 'Still, it won't be so much fun.' Her sympathetic expression had begun to change into a childish pout.

'We'll do something exciting ourselves. Something wild and carefree.' Lucy threw her arms above her head and looked to the ceiling for inspiration. 'We'll go riding over the moors. I knew there was a perfect answer. Chloe will come. Chloe loves riding.'

'Chloe's been up for ages. She said she woke up early and couldn't get back to sleep.'

'Darling Chloe's rather on edge at the moment.'

'I thought I might wash my hair.' Eliza's expression was now definitely sulky.

'It'll dry beautifully on horseback. Now, darling, nip off while I come to myself.'

Eliza left the room reluctantly like a child dismissed. It seemed to her that Lucy was already very much herself.

*

It was a wild day. Not grey and thunderous like the day before but hesitating fitfully between sunshine and rain which were swung one before the other by the high wild wind.

As far as Lucy was concerned, it qualified as a beautiful day. Her high spirits were in hysterical contrast to the lassitude of the night before. She arranged for three horses to be prepared for them at the local riding stables and slotted a studded leather belt through her purple corduroy trousers.

'Why am I always more energetic than my guests!' she cried laughingly as she set out from the house with Chloe and Eliza.

*

The shoot had already been in progress for several hours, but even though game was not scarce the bag was so far disappointing. At about the time Lucy and her captives were climbing onto their uncombed mounts, the guns were strung out in a curving line before a smallish coppice. Ahead of them the beaters were cracking the trees with their sticks and preparing to make their weird battle cries.

Alex, as one of the best shots, was at the very end of the line, slightly ahead of Tom who stood next to him. Their host, Dundalk, was at the other end and between them several of his own guests, Teddy and Dundalk's seventeen-year-old son, who stood next to Tom. He was rather unsure of himself and kept peering nervously at his trigger as if he feared it might go off without his finger pressing it.

'This is always a good place,' he shouted to Tom, in order to restore his self-confidence.

'Good. Good,' said Tom, and then turning his back, called to Alex. 'Your turn for first, I think. I hear it's a good place.'

Meanwhile at the other end of the line Dundalk was making arrangements for their lunch break. This would be the last drive of the morning. When it was over and the dogs had dragged in the carcasses, they would go to his well-ordered hunting lodge and feed off roast saddle of lamb.

Suddenly the beaters struck up in an unearthly chorus.

*

The three women had been galloping over the springy heather. Lucy led, her yellow hair blowing in ringlets behind her and her face whipped into a kind of exultant smile. They were separated from the shoot by the steep hillside and a second small coppice below it, so that the strange noise from the beaters only came up to them slightly muffled above the noise of their horses' hooves.

Lucy pulled in her horse till he was completely still. She dropped the reins onto his wet and panting neck and appeared to be listening intently. Chloe and Eliza followed her example. Almost at once there was a loud and continuing volley of gunfire. Then as suddenly as it had started it was finished.

Lucy sighed. She unclenched her fingers which had been wound among her horse's mane. Red marks were drawn across the back of her hand.

'I'm thinking of joining the anti-blood-sport league.' Chloe flapped a rein idly across her horse's shoulder.

'They're vermin,' Lucy turned on her fiercely.

'That's foxes. Not pheasants.'

'It's sinister, though, isn't it?' Eliza shivered. 'The way everything's so quiet now. As if it was a battlefield and they're counting the dead.'

'It is. And they are.' Chloe had woken in a perverse unsettled humour which was not improved by Lucy's uncompromising energy.

'It's starting to rain,' said Lucy suddenly. And as if at her command a flurry of water blew across their faces. Chloe looked up and was surprised to see how dark it had become.

'Oh, no. Not again.'

'And my hair had just dried,' Eliza wailed.

'We'd better go back.' Lucy wheeled her horse round

165

but instead of going back the same way they had come, she set off down a different track which led towards the shoot.

'Here, wait for us!' Eliza cried, kicking her less eager horse.

*

Reynolds and Philippa had decided to work up an appetite for lunch. They strode out of the house in sensible macintoshes and borrowed gum boots. They thought they might walk up to meet the riders or even catch a whiff of the shoot and indeed they heard the last faraway volley of gunfire. But they were quite unprepared for the sight that met their eyes as they climbed out of the woodland and onto a stretch of wide-open moor.

The two parties were about to converge. The three figures on horseback walked slowly down across the vast expanse, like some tiny frieze off an urn. Coming from the left was a longer procession, though less well outlined, as they were on foot and in long grass.

The scene appeared through a thin veil of rain. But even so, Reynolds could see quite clearly that a long rectangular object, about the length of a man, was being carried in their midst. Reynolds said,

'I think there's been an accident.'

Philippa gave a shriek, 'No! Oh, no. How ghastly!'

*

Lucy rode up to the men who carried the body. But her horse snorted through flared nostrils and stamped his feet. He wouldn't go near to death.

'I shot him,' Tom said, as if he was repeating what he had said several times before.

Dundalk, their host, ran round wringing his hands and crying out over and over again,

'What a tragedy. What a terrible accident. What a misfortune.' Every now and again, he gave a nervous look at his son who was as white as the corpse. He was plagued by the dread that it had been his son's unpractised hand, and not Tom's experienced one, that had fired the fatal shot.

'Alex! Alex!' Eliza suddenly burst out, as if it had taken all this time to realize what she was seeing.

Lucy stood over her lover's body and looked at the mess of blood spreading across his chest. Her eyes were dry.

'I shot him,' said Tom in his curious flat manner.

'The most dreadful thing,' said Teddy, whose pink face was unsuited to tragedy.

'Alex! What's happened? Alex! I don't understand,' Eliza shrieked and threw herself off her horse. Chloe dismounted quietly. There was something about the situation that filled her with such horror, that she felt if she allowed herself any emotion she would go mad. She mustn't think about what it all meant. She mustn't understand. She took Eliza's arm and stopped her throwing herself over Alex.

One of the beaters took the reins of the three horses which were becoming more and more restless and led them a little way away.

'I didn't see it,' said Dundalk's son appealingly, although no one listened to him. 'I didn't see it. I was looking down.'

'Terrible accident. What a misfortune. Such a dreadful thing to happen. Never known it.' Dundalk ran round to each of them in turn.

Eliza began to wail. It was an awful piercing cry that made the beaters look uncomfortably at each other, as if one of their dogs was misbehaving.

Lucy turned round from the body and pointed out Eliza to Dundalk. Her voice was quiet and calm.

'Can you take him to your house? My daughter's hysterical, you see. We can't bring him to our house.'

'Quite. Quite. Yes. I do see. Of course. Anything I can do to help. The police of course . . . The doctor.'

'He's dead,' said Lucy.

'Yes. Quite.' Dundalk was glad to have something to do and began to give orders. The bearers turned round and prepared to move in another direction.

Chloe left Eliza and went into the middle of the little group.

'Tom,' she said, 'what have you done?'

Tom looked at her and they faced each other across the flat pale face of Alex. Tom's look was steadfast. Although he seemed in a state of shock, there was no nervousness about him.

'I shot him,' he said. 'I'm sorry, Chloe.'

'Worst accident. Absolutely the worst accident . . .'

Once more there were two processions separating across the moors.

Lucy put her arm through her husband's and they began to walk slowly back towards the house. They seemed unaware of anyone else around them.

'Mummy! Mummy!' Eliza shrieked behind them.

Lucy put out her free arm and Eliza ran into it, as if seeking shelter.

'Darling,' Lucy said, as she walked between the two of them, her husband and her daughter.

Reynolds, who walked behind them, thought that against the black and thunderous sky they had an ancient dignity about them, as if they had stepped from some Greek tragedy. The whole affair impressed him with the majesty of the inevitable. Tom was such a quiet man to be the centre of a drama, so restrained, so English. But then even that was wrong, for he was really Scottish. Reynolds turned for a moment and looked at the wild hillside behind them.

EPILOGUE

The sky was such a brilliant blue that the eye was too dazzled for more than a quick glance and then must turn away. The sun with rays like glass lit up Lucy's special roses, that started a deep gold in the centre and spread along the petals from a creamy yellow to a glowing pink at the furled tips, so that her guests couldn't help seeing in them a reflection of her own glorious colouring. They wove along a trellis in her London garden and dipped gracefully over trios of tall white lilies.

It was Sunday afternoon and the whole garden was filled with that delicious sense of doing nothing and yet being part of something perfect.

At the far end of the lawn Ticky was doing a puzzle with her nanny. The green grass, though neatly clipped, was springy and the pieces kept breaking apart as if they had a life of their own.

'Oh. Oh.' Ticky pounced delightedly on another. 'They jump about like frogs.'

Rupert, who had just had a birthday, was stretched flat on his tummy, so deeply engrossed in a comic annual he'd been given that he could not even spare the time to swot a fly that was parading across his bare back.

Eliza was at first a pair of long golden legs, for she was on the terrace and half-hidden by a stone urn from which sweet peas climbed in energetic disarray. Eliza was sun-bathing; she wore the smallest of bikinis and her limbs were lightly oiled. Over her eyes she had placed two shiny leaves from a camelia bush above her head. It gave her upturned face a blank statue's beauty.

Above her and to the right sat Lucy. She was dressed all in white and her face was shaded by a large straw hat. She sat on the swing seat and pushed it gently to and fro. Her expression was meditative and yet vibrant, as if she expected something or someone.

Tom looked down on his family. He was sitting at his desk in his study which faced over the garden. The sun glinted on the window so that from the outside no one could have seen his expression.

There was a slight clatter from the french windows that led out from the drawing-room to the terrace, and a man's figure appeared. He stood at the top of the steps for a moment and took in the beauty of the scene before him.

Then Lucy saw him.

'Reynolds!' she cried.

Eliza twitched her head at the sound, so that the leaves slid from her eyes.

At the same time the sun was captured by the smallest of puffy white clouds and in that dim second Tom's face appeared from behind the glass. He was smiling.

More about Penguins and Pelicans

Penguinews, which appears every month, contains details of all the new books issued by Penguins as they are published. From time to time it is supplemented by *Penguins in Print*, which is our complete list of almost 5,000 titles.

A specimen copy of *Penguinews* will be sent to you free on request. Please write to Dept EP, Penguin Books Ltd, Harmondsworth, Middlesex, for your copy.

In the U.S.A.: For a complete list of books available from Penguins in the United States write to Dept CS, Penguin Books, 625 Madison Avenue, New York, New York 10022.

In Canada: For a complete list of books available from Penguins in Canada write to Penguin Books Canada Ltd, 2801 John Street, Markham, Ontario L3R 1B4.

The Great Railway Bazaar

Paul Theroux

Paul Theroux set out one day with the intention of boarding every train that chugged into view from Victoria Station in London to Tokyo Central – and so began a hugely entertaining railway odyssey.

Evelyn Waugh

Christopher Sykes

'It is definitely not to be missed if you are interested in Evelyn Waugh, his work, the art of biography, or even the personality of one of our great English eccentrics' – Antonia Fraser

The Liners

Terry Coleman

The liners of the North Atlantic run, with their opulent luxury and fabulous clientele, fired the imagination of millions in their day. Terry Coleman stokes the flame anew with this beautiful book.

Superwoman

Shirley Conran

'This historic volume' (as the *Guardian* put it) is a practical guide to running a home in ways that minimize the chores and save time and money. It is aimed especially at women who have to combine that job with earning a living outside the home.

The Family Arsenal

Paul Theroux

A novel of urban terror and violence set in the grimy decay of South-East London.

'One of the most brilliantly evocative novels of London that has appeared for years ... very disturbing indeed' – Michael Ratcliffe in *The Times*

Billy Liar on the Moon

Keith Waterhouse

'I beg you, read this brilliant book. Even if you have to steal it' – *Sunday Mirror*

Billy Liar is back, older but not wiser. And his fantasies have come home to roost in the awful concrete jungle of Shepford. Surrounded by a wife, rat-faced neighbours, scheming rivals at work, and a lovely, sexy mistress whose tongue can do things Billy hasn't even thought of, he struggles with his *alter ego*, Oscar, to attain a semblance of adulthood.

The Penguin Dorothy Parker

The Penguin Dorothy Parker includes stories and poems published collectively in 1944; later uncollected stories, articles and reviews; and the contents of *Constant Reader* (her *New Yorker* book reviews) – in all of which she sharpens her legendary wits on the foibles of others.